1888
Mission

The innovative 1888 Center, located in the Historic District of Old Towne Orange, California, is a bookstore, gallery, workshop and café serving Contra Coffee & Tea. Our goal as a nonprofit organization is to provide our diverse neighborhoods with curated content and lifelong learning programs that are educational and entertaining.

Through storytelling, we synergize the creative efforts of individuals to provide essential tools for cultural and civic enrichment—empathy, opportunity, and a collaborative network.

1888 Center programs are recorded and archived as a free educational resource on our website or with your favorite podcast app including Apple and Spotify. Each interdisciplinary episode of the 1888 Center Podcast is designed to provide a unique platform for industry innovators to share stories about art, literature, music, history, science, or technology.

1888

Novellas

1. Corrie Greathouse, *Another Name for Autumn*
2. Ryan Gattis, *The Big Drop: Homecoming*
3. Jon Frechette, *The Frontman*
4. Richard Gaffin, *Oneironautics*
5. Ryan Gattis, *The Big Drop: Impermanence*
6. Alex Sargeant, *Sci-Fidelity*
7. Veronica Bane, *Mara*
8. Kevin Staniec, *Begin*
9. Arianna Basco, *Palms Up*
10. Douglas Cowie, *Sing for Life: Tin Pan Alley*
11. Tomas Moniz, *Bellies and Buffalos*
12. Brett Arnold, *Avalon, Avalon*
13. Douglas Cowie, *Sing for Life: Away, You Rolling River*
14. Pam Jones, *The Biggest Little Bird*
15. Peppur Chambers, *Harlem's Awakening*
16. Kate St. Clair, *Spelled*
17. Veronica Bane, *Miyuki*
18. William Brandon, *Silence*
19. J.T. Robertson, *The Memory Thieves*
20. Scott Alumbaugh, *Will Kill for Food*
21. Shaunn Grulkowski, *Retcontinuum*
22. Kate St. Clair, *Cursed*
23. B. Tanner Fogle, *A Little Evil*
24. Nate Ragolia, *There You Feel Free*
25. Cazzey Louis Cereghino, *116* Days with Dad*
26. Nate Pensky, *Skinny Blue*
27. Jason L. Pyrz, *Renaissance Spook*
28. Scott Amstadt, *Foster*
29. Jon-Barrett Ingels, *How to Succeed by Failing*
30. Jordan A. Rothacker, *The Pit, and No Other Stories*
31. Chanda J. Grubbs, *Albedo*

32. Khristian Mecom, *Love & Black Holes*

33. Eric Z. Weintraub, *Dreams of an American Exile*

34. Dean Moses, *A Stalled Ox*

35. Shannon Barnsley, *Beneath Blair Mountain*

36. Allison A. Spector, *Let's Stalk Rex Jupiter*

37. Ryan Dunlap, *The Goldfish*

38. Danielle M. Walters, *Cut the Thread*

39. Taryn Tilton, *Cherry Cherry*

40. Kathy Joy, *Last One To The Bridge*

41. Kevin Staniec, *And Then, This*

42. Abbey Lenzie, *In The Desert*

THE PLAZA LITERARY PRIZE
National Novella Competition

The Plaza Literary Prize is a national novella competition. We believe a great story is never defined by its length and welcome all genres and themes with compelling characters and evocative moments. We're looking for our generation's Hemingway, Oates, or Steinbeck.

The City of Orange, California was incorporated on April 6, 1888. The center of the town became known as the Plaza, which has become a symbol of the community and a catalyst for storytelling.

THE PLAZA LITERARY PRIZE
2018 Jury

The Plaza Literary Prize welcomes our 2018 Jury–Jonathan Alexander, Panio Gianopoulos, Namrata Poddar, Irena Praitis, and Héctor Tobar–an inspiring panel of authors, editors, journalists, and professors.

Jonathan Alexander is a writer, literacy scholar, and cultural critic. The author, co-author or editor of thirteen books, he is Chancellor's Professor of English and Informatics at the Universityu of California, Irvine, where he also serves as the Founding Director of the Center of Excellence in Writing & Communication. He is the YA editor and a frequent contributor of the Los Angeles Review of Books.

Panio Gianopoulos is the author of the story collection, *How to Get Into Our House and Where We Keep the Money,* and the novella, *A Familiar Beast.* His stories, essays, and poetry have appeared in *Tin House, Northwest Review, Salon, The Rattling Wall, Chicago Quarterly Review, Big Fiction, The Brooklyn Rail, Catamaran Literary Reader,* and the *Los Angeles Review of Books.* A recipient of a New York Foundation for the Arts Award for Non-Fiction, he has been included in the anthologies *The Bastart on the Couch, Cooking and Stealing: The Tin House Non-Fiction Reader,* and *The Encyclopedia of Exes.*

Namrata Poddar writes fiction, non-fiction, occasionally translates Francophone writers of Afro-Asian diaspora into English and serves as Interviews Editor for *Kweli* where she curates a series on Race, Power, and Storytelling. For over a decade, her work has explored the intersection of storytelling and social justice via race, class, gender, place and migration. Her creative work has appeared in *The Margins, Transition, Literary Hub, Electric Literature, Los Angeles Review of Books Quarterly, The Feminist Wire, Necessary Fiction, Longreads (forthcoming)* and elsewhere. As a literary critic, her work on islands and coastal cultures have appeared in English and in French in anthologies on the Caribbean, Pacific, and Indian Ocean across the world. She holds a Ph.D. in French Studies from the University of Pennsylvania, an MFA in fiction from Bennington Writing Seminars, and Andrew W. Mellon Postdoctoral Fellowship in Transnational Cultures from UCLA where she taught contemporary multiethnic literature in the departments of English, African, Global, French & Francophone Studies and Honors Collegium. She has lived in different parts of the world and currently calls Huntington Beach home.

Irena Praitis's fifth book *The Last Stone in the Circle* received the 2015 Red Mountain Press Poetry Poetry Prize. Her poems, translations, essays, and reviews have appeared in more than 100 journals including *Southwest Review, Denver Quarterly,* and *Rattle*. She was a Fulbright Scholar in Vilnius, Lithuania, and is a professor of creative writing and literature at California State University, Fullerton. She lives in Fullerton, California, with her son Ishaan.

Héctor Tobar is the Lost Angeles-born author of four books, including the novels *The Tattooed Soldier* and *The Barbarian Nurseries*. His non-fiction *Deep Down Dark: The Untold Stories of Thirty-Three Men Buried in a Chilean Mine and the Miracle that Set Them Free*, was a finalist for the National Book Critics Circle Award and the Los Angeles Times Book Prize: it was also a New York Times bestseller and adapted into the film *The 33*. *The Barbarian Nurseries* was a New York Times Notable Book and won the California Book Award Gold Medal for fiction. Tobar's fiction has also appeared in *Zyzzyva* and in *Best American Short Stories* 2016. He earned his MFA in Creative Writing from the University of California, Irvine, and has taught writing and journalism at Pomona College and the University of Oregon; he is currently an associate professor at UC Irvine. As a journalist, he was a foreign correspondent with the Los Angeles Times in Buenos Aires and Mexico City, and a part of the reporting team that earned a Pulitzer Prize for coverage of the 1992 Los Angeles riots. Tobar has also been an op-ed writer for the New York Times and a contributor to the New Yorker. He is the son of Guatemalan immigrants.

IN THE DESERT
Abbey Lenzie

1

On his last days, Cole's lips have been like the scorched earth of the desert. Jael pinches a piece of wet ice, rubbing it softly on his cracked lips, and he exhales with the small relief. He spends his days fading in and out of the world. He swims to the surface, disoriented and hazy, only to pass out again when the pain swells to a peak.

It started out slow. A wet cough rooted at the bottom of his lungs. He would wake up in the middle of the night hacking, and Jael would roll over and place her hand on his chest, watching him grimace.

And yet, he would insist it was just a cough. He managed to hide the blood for a solid two weeks before Jael found flecks of red on his pillow one day when she was doing the wash. She forced Cole to go to the Healer the next day.

They traveled to the town on the other side of the canyon under the hot summer sun, every penny of next year's crop money in their pockets. The Healer had nothing that could help. Usually, he said, the leftover radiation from the fallout didn't get you until you were older—at least 50—but Cole, he said, was just early. He took most of their money, patted Cole on the shoulder, and sent them home to "wait it out."

The months stretched on, unending, and Cole could no longer pull himself out of bed. Planting season came and went unnoticed, and their farm grew over with purple thistles and wheatgrass. Another year passed. While Jael watched, he dissipated like smoke until there was little left. Just watery skin holding eggshell bones, and the ever, ever present cough.

Gradually, something in his eyes shifted.

When she looks at them now, they are empty. Black and empty, like the bottom of a well.

It is now that she makes her decision.

Or in her mind, it is made for her.

She finds her solace in the cool silver edge of a knife and in the warm crimson blood that flows so fast.

* * *

After it is done, she sits in the chair as night comes. They live on the far edge of the canyon, right up against the mesa wall. There are no neighbors, no friends, no family. No one. Her hand rests on top of his, and she watches the color drain from his skin like the blue drains from the sky at the end of a long day. At some point she realizes that his hand has gotten cold, and she pulls hers away with a shiver. The thick scent of iron chokes the air.

She's always heard that when a person dies their loved ones can feel the soul leave the room, and she waits for that feeling. Through her vigil that night, she waits for the sense of relief, but it never comes.

When the moon shines its light through the window, she takes his cold hand again.

"It's over now," she tells him. She brushes his hair back from his face.

She stands up and goes over to the window, snapping the curtains shut, cutting off the pale iridescent light. She squints at him in the dark. "You can go."

She walks slowly back and forth across the length of the room, casting a glance at him each time she passed the foot of his bed. Their bed. Her bed.

A headache starts to build at the base of her skull, radiating up, and her vision turns red around the edges. She looks around the house, its dirt floor and ramshackle walls, and it is full of him. Every plate and cloth and scrap in that place reminds her of him. That pile of beans—the green beans over there—he brought those in from the garden one day. He spent an hour stacking them in that funny pile, and they were going to cook them, but the next day he tripped on his own foot, and he couldn't get up off the floor. Now they are just sitting there on the table rotting, and for months she couldn't find a way to move them because she knew if she touched them, she would feel like she was touching his hand, and she couldn't do that anymore. So, they lay there still: soft and blue-green from the mold that covers them.

The memory knocks the wind out of her, and she crumples on the ground, leaning against the wall, breathing hard. She cries until her body runs out of salt and water, and then she cries without tears until she passes out without realizing it somewhere just before dawn.

The first thing she feels when she opens her eyes is confusion. Then the memory comes crashing down. The blood—she can still smell it, can still see the too-dark stain in the dirt—makes her gag. She covers her nose with her hand and gathers what she knows she'll need: food, blanket, knife. She pulls a small box from under the bed and holds it in her lap for a moment. Then she opens it quickly, like ripping off a bandage. Inside is a slim gold chain threaded through a clear, round diamond. She latches the necklace around her neck and tucks it under her shirt, leaving the now empty box where it lies.

She opens the door but pauses in the doorway, one foot in and one foot out. In front of her, the world is still waking up. The sun has scarcely touched the far canyon wall; it won't creep down to reach the house for many hours yet. She'll be long gone by then. Across the canyon, through the pass, and into the desert.

And yet. The weight of everything behind her is too heavy. She turns back to face the house.

She sees the matchbook, sitting beside the stove. Then it's in her hand, and she drags her thumb across the black, gritty strip. Her head throbs as she looks around the empty and full house. This is all that is left.

Her mother used to say that to strike a match is to unsheathe a weapon. In the dry grasslands of the desert, fire burns with insatiable speed. The wind picks it up eagerly and drags it for miles, and it goes willingly, consuming everything in its path until nothing is left but ash.

Matches are not as meek as they seem, little Jael, her mother would say.

With level eyes and a steady hand, she strikes her first match.

2

In the center of town, the one-armed girl peers out from behind her curtain of wild strawberry hair. Around the corner, she sees the bakery. It's a two-story building, one of the few left standing after the dust settled so many decades ago. It has huge window frames that sit open and empty and a corner that looks like someone took a bite out of it. On the cracked sidewalk in front, an old man sits in a rusty metal chair. *He's actually a very old man*, Agi thinks. He has a big belly and a wide, white mustache. The man's gaze drifts toward the end of the street, and Agi ducks back behind the corner.

"Is he there?" Kids jostle her on all sides. Their clothes are ragged and ill fitting, and only a few of them wear shoes.

Agi looks at the big one. Kirt. He's a good head-and-shoulders taller than the rest of them, which makes him the leader by default. "You know, we could just ask," she says scathingly.

Kirt arches an eyebrow. He's got a pointy nose and a pointy chin and pointy elbows that are good for jabbing. "Sure. We'll just go up to him and say, 'Excuse me, can we have—'" He pretends to count the handful of kids, "like twenty loaves of bread?" He punctuates this by spitting on the ground.

Agi purses her lips. "Well, no, not all of us at once." She peeks around the corner again. The street is lined with rusted old cars, long since picked over for scraps, and the old man has his feet propped up on the frame of one. "But he looks nice. Maybe if we go one at a time and ask real nice and spread it out over a few days."

"Don't be an idiot. Just distract him while I sneak in," Kirt says.

At the other end of the block, a tall man with wide shoulders turns the corner. He's dressed in gray from the top of his helmet to the bottom of his steel-toed boots. Agi whips behind the wall.

"Guard," she says.

Kirt peers around the corner and then jabs Agi in the side with his elbow. "Hope you're a fast runner, then."

Agi shakes her head. "No way. Look, I'm telling you, just give me five minutes. I can get him to give me a couple loaves." She pokes a finger in Kirt's chest. "Wait. Here."

Before he can say anything, Agi is off. Halfway down the street, she checks over her shoulder. A dozen wide eyes and two very angry ones stare at her. She turns back to the old man, who is now watching her approach.

She pulls up her biggest grin. "Hi, I'm Agi."

His eyes narrow.

"Nice day?" she asks.

"What do you want?"

"Nothing," Agi says with a shrug. "Just looking."

Agi peers up at the roof of the shop. Rusting metal beams hold everything up, sagging in the middle. "Shoo," she whistles, "This is an old one isn't it?"

He twists his neck to look at the building. "It is."

"Were you here before?"

The man nods.

Agi's mouth drops. "No way." She points to the shop. "Here? Right here in this same building?"

The man sits a little straighter. "I was a jeweler then. Finest one in town."

Agi tilts her head. "You sold jewelry?"

The man stands up and starts inside. Agi follows.

"So, you sold jewelry?" she asks again, a little louder.

He cuts his eyes to her, watching her for a moment. She just smiles. "Made it, too," he says finally. "Rubies, emeralds, diamonds, sapphires. Sold them in big glass cases." He gestures to the square stands around the shop, now serving as tables for loaves of bread, each a mirror image of the next. "There used to be glass on all of these." He shifts a light brown loaf absentmindedly from one place to another.

"Bet you made a ton of money off all that after the fallout."

The man shakes his head.

Agi's cheeks flush. Of course. "Looted?" she asks.

He doesn't say anything, but he doesn't have to. Agi tries to picture it, all those jewels sparkling on the counters instead of the plain brown ovals of bread. "I bet they were pretty."

The man turns to look at her. There's an odd expression on his face, and Agi can't tell if he's sad or happy. She looks down at her shoes.

"Radiation?" he tilts his head to her bony shoulder stump.

Agi nods.

He shakes his head, turning away, and mutters something about what the world has come to.

"Listen," she says, pushing her hair out of her face, "I was thinking maybe I could sweep up in here a little. You wouldn't have to pay me money, just some bread every couple days or so."

The man's eyes jump to something over Agi's shoulder. She turns just in time to see Kirt leap through the empty window frame, a dozen loaves tucked into his arms. He lands awkwardly and drops a couple on the sidewalk. He turns and smirks at Agi. "Grab those for me?"

Then he's gone, that horrible smirk burned into Agi's vision. She turns slowly to look at the baker. His face shifts impressively fast from shock to rage.

"I wasn't part of that, I swear!" Her voice comes out squeaky. "I don't even know him!"

The old man storms past her, through the door, and looks up and down the sidewalk. Agi trails after him.

"Okay, I know him, but I only met him last week, I swear! And he's a jerk! I told him I wasn't going to help. I did! I promise!"

The man finds who he's looking for. Across the street, the Guard is leaning against a busted streetlight. When the baker raises one finger into the air, the man in gray's eyes are drawn to it like magnets. The old man points first at Kirt's retreating back, and then he lowers his hand and points at Agi. The Guard nods.

For a moment, Agi hopes desperately that he will go for Kirt first. "Come on," she mutters. "He deserves it anyways."

Then Kirt whips around a corner and out of sight. The Guard walks toward her. Agi takes one last look at the old man. His eyes are furious and unrelenting.

The Guard, his tan skin clashing with his gray clothes, is already halfway across the street.

Agi runs. The ground is uneven beneath her feet, but she knows how to handle it. She jumps over the cracks in the sidewalk and piles of broken bricks. Behind her, she hears the heavy thudding of the Guard's boots. She turns into an alley just past an empty building that reads Cof-ee –ous- in chipped silver letters above. His footsteps pound close behind her. He's fast.

She makes a mental note to punch Kirt's face in if she ever sees him again. Two more minutes and she could have gotten the bread. The old man was pretty nice, after all. But then she pictures Kirt being dragged away by a Guard and decides that's punishment enough. People like him always get caught in the end.

Agi pops out of the alley onto a main street, wide enough for four cars side by side. It's packed bumper-to-bumper with rusted old cars that haven't moved an inch since their last desperate attempt at evacuation. Agi hops over hoods and between doors. She checks over her shoulder again. The Guard is struggling to squeeze between two big trucks. Agi smiles. Not for the first time, she thanks her lucky stars for being born so small.

Turning back around, she runs right smack into a second Guard. The force throws her backwards and she falls flat on her back, the wind knocked out of her. The new Guard pulls her up by her wrist while she's still catching her breath.

"What do we have here?" he asks, peering down at her.

The first Guard finally catches up. He puts his hands on his knees, panting. "Thanks," he says.

"What'd she do?" the new Guard says.

The first straightens up. "Stole from a baker."

"I did not! I didn't take a single thing from him," Agi says.

"We'll see about that."

The Guard searches her roughly, shoving his hands in her pockets and yanking off her shoes and shaking them upside down.

"Get off me! I told you I don't have anything."

"That's too bad," the second Guard muses. "Could'a gotten you a free pass."

The first Guard drops her to the ground. "So, we have two options for thieves in this town," he says. "We can lock you up for, oh, what do you say? Five years?" He looks to his colleague.

Agi shoves her feet back into her shoes, sniffling.

The second guard smiles and nods. "Sounds about right."

"Right. Or you can make sure we never see you in this town again. The desert's pretty brutal, though, so choose wisely." He grins.

Agi grits her teeth. "Nobody's going to lock me up."

The Guard shrugs. "Have it your way. But listen," he pulls her close, his hot breath hitting her, "If I catch you here again, it won't be a simple lock up, you hear?"

"The guard dogs have gotta eat, too," the second Guard chimes in.

Agi jerks free from his grasp and runs, their laughs chasing after her.

* * *

It's not the first time she's been thrown out of a town, and it's not likely to be the last. She gathers her wits about her, cursing Kirt even harder with every step, and heads off into the desert. Soon, she finds the river that runs along the edge of town, and she follows its winding, snaking path across the canyon. Up ahead, the canyon pass looms before her like a great doorway. She's not sure what's through it, but it has to be better than what's she's leaving behind.

3

The fire is sudden and sure and dangerous, and that seems fitting. The scent of alcohol is heavy in the air, and it grabs the fire before the match even hits the ground. Flames rush in a straight line from Jael's feet to the base of the house where they gnaw on the rough wood. The wind picks up the fire, tossing it higher, and the warped glass window cracks and glitters and crashes and then is gone.

It is a steady fire, full of the dense black smoke of so many things burning. Jael watches it and sighs. The smoke makes her eyes sting, but she doesn't turn away. If she could get any closer, she would, but she can already feel the heat on her forehead, so she stays where she is. She thinks about sitting down, but then thinks better of it. She has to be ready to run.

So instead she stands. The flames are mesmerizing— faster than a dust storm or a rattlesnake's tail. Jael can scarcely track the movement with her eyes, one flame blending into the next, and she makes herself dizzy trying. The brightness of it burns into her vision, but still she can't look away. She watches as the fire consumes her past.

4

Something about Jael gives Haskell pause. Something about the way she stands there, facing the fire, doing nothing to stop it. She watches it with her head tilted like she's trying to understand something.

Haskell hides behind the leaning garden shed and tries to understand it, too.

One thing's for certain: Cole must have finally kicked the bucket. After considering for a moment, Haskell decides this doesn't have to throw a wrench in his plan. Actually, as long as she hasn't sold it yet, this might make things easier. Haskell covers his mouth with his shirt to keep out the smoke as he runs through his lines in his head. *I'm so sorry for your loss. I just wish I could have made it in time to say goodbye. We're family; we have to stick together now.*

The question is what to do about the fire? Maybe it started by accident and the woman's still in shock? He could run in and play the hero. Surely that would win him some points.

Then, from the road, someone shouts. Jael's head whips toward the noise. In half a breath, she grabs her bag from the ground and disappears into a patch of Pinyon pines. *Startled like a rabbit*, Haskell thinks with a chuckle. He waits a few minutes before jogging after her.

He follows her tracks easily through the gnarled pines, and then later past a stand of orange trees that takes him by surprise. But then again, everything about this canyon takes him by surprise. There are pockets of shade from the canyon walls, and he even hears the gentle *whoosh* of a river. Unfortunately, it's coming from somewhere behind him.

He groans as he realizes she's heading away from the river, straight for the desert. He can't imagine anyone wanting to leave this place—unless they were running from something. As he jogs along, his mind turns and turns over the secret he now knows, and how he can best use it.

5

Jael stands silhouetted against the heat of the glaring sun. The wind tugs at her coarse black hair, snaking a few wispy strands out of the knot at the base of her neck. Beads of sweat drip down her back, and she squints at the pillar of smoke in the distance through a haze of heat. It's climbing up high in the blue, casting a look of clouds about the place, though the day is hot and clear.

She went the long way around the canyon to avoid the town and all its busybodies, but she's finally through the canyon pass. The road stretches in front of her, sun-cracked and bumpy from decades of decay. Broken slabs of cement jut up in her path, and Jael walks to the side of the road. She veers around a dusty green sign lying on the road, indicating the town behind her.

Her heart pounds as she looks at the great expanse of land before her, and she's glad she put on her sturdy boots this morning. They're light brown leather, soft but thick. Yellow road dust nestles into the cracks in the leather as she puts right foot in front of left and left in front of right, over and over. Her shirt is thin and white to protect from the heat, but still it sticks to the sweat along the top of her back.

She sets her jaw forward, her eyes resolutely straight, and refuses to look at the smoke that she can still feel in her lungs. She exhales and pictures her aching lungs, ash covered and black, squeezing out the smoke like an oily washcloth being wrung out. Soon enough, she'll be through the pass and the smoke will be behind her for good.

As the hours steal away, her mind tries to wander, but she doesn't let it. She pushes her legs harder, forcing her mind to focus on her body. Only the walking. Think of nothing else.

And it works. With her mind on her journey, she doesn't hear the man walking behind her until he calls out.

"Jael?"

She whips around and stops in her tracks. He is short and stocky with shoulder-length brown hair. His travel bag is small, and he holds it loosely over one shoulder. Jael can't see a weapon, but still she holds her knife ready in her hand.

"Jael?" he says again. "Are you Jael?" He walks a few steps closer but pulls up short when he sees her knife.

"Who are you?" Jael asks.

He puts his palms out in a placating gesture and walks toward her. "I'm sorry. I didn't mean to scare you. I'm not going to hurt you."

Jael takes a step closer with her knife pointed at him. "I know you're not."

He stops walking. "Look, maybe I got the wrong person. Is your name Jael?"

She looks at him. She's sure she's never seen this man before, but there's something about him…something familiar. "Who are you?"

His hands drop to his sides. "My name is Haskell," he says. "I'm Cole's brother."

Jael's face remains clear, but the hand holding her knife tenses. The man—Haskell—notices it.

"You are Jael, aren't you?"

She stares at him.

He tries again. "We fell out a long time ago, me and Cole. I don't even know if he mentioned me." His voice tilts like he's asking a question.

"He did." Her voice is quiet.

When she doesn't say anything else, he walks a step closer, but Jael backs away, keeping the distance between them.

"Listen, I heard Cole was sick and—"

"What do you want?" Her eyes are hard.

"I—What do you mean?"

She says each word slowly, "What do you want?"

"I just wanted to let you know I'm here. I heard the news and came to—"

Jael shakes her head, cutting him off. "No," she says to him. "Why are you here?"

Haskell's mouth gapes open. "I… I guess I just wanted to make sure you were okay."

"I'm fine," she says to him.

She catches his eye and realizes what was so familiar about him when she first saw him. It was the eyes, of course. She looks away.

"Well, good," he says. "I'm glad to hear that." He looks out at the landscape around them. The dry brittlebush crowds their feet and fills in the gaps in the broken pavement. Up ahead, in the distance, great sandstone pillars tower to the sky. His eyes skim unseeing over it all, and he shakes his hair behind his shoulders. "Is there anything at all I can do to help?"

Jael turns around and starts down the road again.

"Wait!" Haskell calls after her. "Where are you going?"

She moves fast, and he has to jog to keep up.

"You can't just leave," he says.

There's a long moment of silence, and then he says, "I'm coming with you."

She stops suddenly, forcing him to pull up short, and looks him square in the eye. "No. You're not."

"We're family. We can help each other." He reaches for her shoulder, but she pulls away.

"You're a complete stranger," she says. "And I don't need your help." With that, she runs.

* * *

Long after she can no longer hear him calling, she keeps running. The stitch in her side gives her something to focus on other than his too-familiar voice. The pain in her legs keeps her from thinking about those eyes.

Only when her legs are numb does she slow. She winds down like a windmill after the wind has passed. When she finally stops, the sun is high overhead and it's fully noon. The hottest part of the day. She sinks to the ground beside a Joshua tree, tucking her knees to her chest to keep them in the small slant of shade.

A thought nags at Jael until she plucks it out and examines it. This is what Cole would want. Someone to be there for her after he was gone. Before things got really bad, she told him over and over that she would be fine. She was fine on her own before him, and she'd be just fine after. She was never bothered by being alone.

"That's what I worry about," he said.

A raven lands a few feet from Jael, and she shoos it away with a wave of her hand. She looks up at the sun, and it glares back at her. Her throat is raw from running, but she emptied her water bottle miles ago, before Haskell found her. She planned on refilling at a gas station turned trading post along the way, but in her panic, she missed the turn-off many miles back.

She rummages through her pack and digs up a hard apple from the bottom. It's still yellow in patches, but it will have to do. She eats it, core and all, in a few big bites, spitting the seeds to the side. The juice from the apple helps a bit, but her head still feels light. Too much running. Too much heat.

The thought comes unbidden into her head.

She knows where she can find water.

She can see the well in her mind, tucked off the path, and the house just behind it. The dirt walls, and wooden furniture, and that ridiculous blue door. Surely someone else moved in after all this time and repainted that awful door. Turquoise, he called it. *Same color as the sky.* And some days, it really was.

She focuses on the well. She can either fill up there or try her luck in the desert. The washes often run empty this time of year. She tells herself it would be stupid to pass the house by. Besides, everything will be different. Nothing will look like it used to. It won't be familiar at all. She tells herself this is a good thing.

6

The rabbit is a lucky strike. Agi has been living in the abandoned house for a few weeks before the old, rusty trap finally catches something. She's gotten used to cooking and skinning animals over the years--tricky with one hand, but not impossible. But still, she's glad this trap is the kind that kills.

The embers in the fire ring are still glowing from last night, so all she has to do is stoke them up a bit and the fire is going again in no time. She sets the jackrabbit on the grate over the flames and heads inside to get a cup for water.

The old house has been good to her so far. It's small, with a main room and a bedroom and a hallway between. It's old enough to be pre-fallout, and the walls shake terribly when the wind blows. To Agi, it's a mansion. Plates and cups and even a few pieces of silverware. Luxuries—the likes of which she hasn't seen in years. A scavenger hunt through the cupboards turned up what she thought might have been a loaf of bread, under the inches of mold, and a pack of something labeled "bubble gum," which turned out to be inedible. She chewed and chewed, but it tasted like sweet rubber. Eventually, she spit it out.

But the best part is the well, deep and cool and just a few hundred feet from the house. A garden sits to the side of the house where, with a little digging under the weeds, she can find potatoes and onions and even a beet once. There's a great, big, twisty Juniper tree behind the house, the kind that's perfect for climbing. It doesn't offer much in terms of shade, but Agi likes the feeling of being up above the world.

When the jackrabbit is cooked all the way through, Agi pushes dirt onto the fire and climbs onto the lowest branch of the Juniper tree. The meat is dry and tastes of smoke, and it's delicious. Agi eats until she feels ready to burst. She has a few dusty Juniper berries for dessert and then lies down in the crook of the branch. The afternoon sun and her full stomach and the soft wind on her face... Her eyelids have never felt so heavy in her life. The sun and the leaves above her cast intricate patterns on the ground below, and in a matter of minutes she is asleep.

7

Above the mud walls, the roof sags wearily, and Jael can see through in spots to the open sky. It looks like a strong gust of wind will detach the whole house from the dust and sand and send it spinning away like a tumbleweed. It was their first house, the only one they could afford.

The porch creaks under Jael's boots. She stops in the doorway. The light blue door is gone. Not repainted, just gone. Jael looks around the yard, but it's nowhere to be seen. She peers through the empty frame and into the house.

He's there.

Standing by the kitchen table.

His hands rhythmically peel a potato. Scrape. Scrape. Scrape.

He looks like he did years ago. Young and strong and straight-shouldered.

Jael tries to move to him, but her muscles are frozen. She tries to call out, and her jaw is locked. Something brushes past her shoulder.

A younger version of herself walks over to him, and he smiles without looking up.

"Good day?"

Her other self shakes her head. Taking a knife from her pocket, she peels another potato vigorously. "People are stingy."

"Money's tight for everyone. You know that," he says. "It's almost winter."

"Exactly."

Cole finishes his potato and sets down the knife. He turns and leans against the table. His hand rests on Jael's arm, and her movements slow.

"It's going to be fine," he says.

Jael standing by the sink says nothing, but Jael standing in the doorway knows what she's thinking. She's thinking of the crates of unsold squash and onions and potatoes sitting in the backyard and of the hundred and one things they need before winter: new blankets, coal, meat, seed.

"Maybe we should go back to the Bower farm," she says finally.

Cole nods to himself for a moment. "Yeah," he says slowly, "We could do that." He walks behind her and closes his arms around her waist. "I know how much you love sharing a house with five other families."

The tension pours out of her.

"Mrs. Bower ringing the wake-up bell at four in the morning."

She turns to face him, his hands sliding to the small of her back.

"Old man Bower playing his cheery little piccolo every day at lunch."

Jael laughs. She takes a step into him and tilts her chin up. He picks up the cue.

Standing in the doorway, Jael feels pressure on her lips. She watches, frozen.

Cole pulls her back toward the bedroom. His hands never leave her, like he's afraid she'll slip away the moment he's no longer touching her. They pass into the hallway and out of sight.

Jael's mind screams at her to follow, to run, but everything is sluggish. She moves in slow motion across the room. When she finally reaches the bedroom, they are gone. The mattress is gray and rotten. When she touches it, she can almost convince herself it's still warm, but of course it's not. A headache throbs where her head meets her neck.

She can hardly breathe. Her eyes lock on the mattress pattern that is achingly familiar: soft yellow leaves intertwining with purple roses. Cole made fun of her endlessly, every time they washed the sheets, for picking such a frilly pattern.

It comes to her in flashes now, all of it tinged with red.

His hand tracing the edge of her chin. Her leg wrapped around his. A soft kiss on her stomach.

"Jael?" His voice comes from behind the tattered curtains.

She runs and rips them aside, but the blank wall stares back at her. She feels a touch on her shoulder and spins around, but there's no one there. A shadow in the hall, but it too is empty.

"Jael?" His voice has an edge of panic.

She runs toward it, but the kitchen is of course empty.

"Jael?" Now it is weak, like the last time she heard it.

"Cole!" She spins around wildly.

"Jael…" It's getting quieter still, barely above a whisper. It comes from the pantry.

"Cole!" She yanks the door open and peers into the dark. She strikes a match—suddenly she's holding a matchbook—and sends the shadows scurrying, but the pantry is empty.

Again. "Jael…"

He's there. Somewhere. He's close. She feels his breath against her neck, but she can't see him. He's so close. She strikes another match and holds it with the first. The flames jump together, joining forces to throw the pantry into sharp contrasts of light and dark. Still, the room is empty.

His voice pricks her ear.

"Jael."

She can't take it. She strikes another match. The room is red. Then another. The fire burns the tips of her fingers, and still, still there's nothing.

It has to go. She has to finish what she started. If she's ever going to be free, it all has to go.

She lays the burning matches on the ground against a crumbling cardboard box, and the flames jump higher. She watches them cross from the box to a low wooden shelf, eating everything along the way.

Only when the highest shelf is roaring with fire does she back out of the pantry and out of the house, coughing. The fire crawls across the floor to the kitchen table. A gentle wind drifts in through the window and coaxes it tenderly toward the back of the house.

Outside, Jael hears nothing. Only the crackle of the fire.

The flames eat up the walls and then move on to the low roof. Soon the whole house will be in flames, and then there will just be ashes. Nothing else.

Jael takes a deep breath and smoke seeps into her lungs.

8

Jael has been walking for a few hours when a snake, coiled in a strike-ready position, hisses at her.

Without moving more than one muscle at a time, she walks backward away from the snake until she is out of its strike zone. The scales on its back make a sticky-sand sound sliding past one another as the snake relaxes its defensive coil.

Jael makes no sound at all when she reaches for her knife and throws it at the snake. The hard silver blade flips over itself in a straight line before it pins the head of the snake to the ground. The desert soaks up the brown blood that gurgles out.

Turning around, Jael leaves the snake to bleed out while she pulls together a fire. She's still got plenty of food in her pack, but there's no need to pass up good meat when it comes by so willingly. When the fire is going, she places a flat stone in the middle.

Jael swings her knife up high and slams it to the ground to split the head off the snake. No sense in trying to get the head meat; if she so much as nicked the venom sacs, the meal could turn deadly. Better to slice it clean off.

The rest of the snake Jael prepares more carefully. She scrapes her blade down the length of its sides and tugs the skin away from the tissue holding it in place. Most of the blood drains away, and whatever is left will boil out when the meat cooks.

She watches it sizzle on the rock until all of the juices are gone and it's just the meat left to char. She flips it over to blacken the other side. Snake meat is tough and even tougher when it's burnt, but at least she will be sure it's cooked all the way through.

Once the meat is tied up in a cloth and stuffed in her bag with the rest of the food, Jael kicks some ash over the embers of the fire and starts off again toward the sun, now a few notches higher above the flat empty horizon.

* * *

In late afternoon, the insects come out. Gnats and flies buzz around her ears. She looks around and, sure enough, sees a small patch of yellow-green cottonwoods just off the road.

She finds the wash early in the evening and stops to make camp for the night. It's shallow, but the water is potable. As she fills up her water jug, she tries not to think about how it makes her trip to the house entirely pointless. So, of course, it's all she thinks about. She strips away her sweat-soaked clothes and rinses them in the water. She lays them out to dry before lowering herself into the shallow, dusty water. It cools her burning skin. This water must have once slid against seashells in the Pacific or under an ancient canoe in a winding river. At some point it was hanging mid-air, hundreds of feet above her head, bumping violently against other water drops to form dark gray clouds.

Taking a deep breath, she lies flat, ducks her head under the surface, and lets the pressure of all the water in the world push against her eardrums. He told her once that he felt like he was drowning. Like the tide was bringing the water level in his lungs higher and higher every day. *If only I were a fish,* he said with a small smile.

Her lungs burn before she breaks the surface to suck in air. She stands and wades out of the water. Dressing while still wet means her clothes stay gloriously damp and cold. She braids her coarse black hair in one long plait and lets it hang cool against her neck, dripping down the center of her back.

Exhaustion comes quickly after all that, and the wetness of her own body lulls her to sleep before the sun has finished sinking out of the sky.

* * *

Jael's dreams that night are not of flames and smoke as she was expecting, but of him.

She's sitting on the edge of his bed. His hand shakes as she holds it lightly, rubbing the tips of his fingers. All of him is shaking, trembling from pain. His eyes are closed, but he's awake. The world isn't kind enough to let him slip into unconsciousness. He moans softly, and his shoulders stiffen.

"Shh, shh. I know." Jael squeezes his hand, and his eyes open suddenly, his gaze erratic.

"Cole. Hey. Focus on me. Can you hear me?" She rubs a circle in his palm, and his eyes slowly shift over to her hand and trace up her arm to finally land on her face.

"Hey," she says.

He looks at her. His eyes are the blackest she's ever seen; black, like looking down the bottom of a well.

Now his breathing is rough. With her hand on his chest, she can feel how each breath is full of jagged air that rubs his lungs raw. When he opens his mouth to say something, all the good air goes out of the room so that now Jael is breathing the jagged-knife air, too. She can't inhale—the walls of her lungs cut open—and her vision turns red around the edges. His hand is slipping, slipping away from her, and she can't hold on because she can't breathe.

In the corner of her eye, something metal catches a glint of light. She hears something snap like a twig.

9

Jael's eyes pop open. It is still night.

Her skin is covered in sweat, chill in the cold open air. She sits up.

The wind is chaos around her. It jumps into her hair and gathers it together to toss it up and down, all around her head. She does nothing to stop it. She curls her arms to her chest, pulling in, tightening, closing, all the while the wind swirling madly around her.

If the feel of the wind means anything to Jael, she doesn't show it.

She tries to shake off the dream. She imagines the remnants of it flying out between the coarse strands of her wild hair. She gives the dream over, letting go, sending it floating out across the desert. She tries. But when the wind finally lays down her hair, it takes nothing with it but dust, and she is alone.

Then she hears it again. A snap. The noise that woke her.

Something is rummaging through the brush.

She freezes. Lying down, she forces her chest to rise and fall in what she hopes will look like a normal rhythm. It's Haskell. He's found her again.

Turning her face to the noise, she can barely make out the outline of something crouching behind the sagebrush. She squints her eyes and can see the shadowy outline of shoulders and a wild mane of hair. A woman, then? There's no doubt in Jael's mind that this woman will kill her for the food in her bag if she's hungry.

Jael forces a sigh and pretends to shift in her sleep, tucking her hand under her blanket to grip the long thin knife that's strapped to her leg.

Then she waits.

After a few minutes, it seems like the woman crouching in the brush is satisfied Jael is asleep because she creeps into the open clearing where Jael lies.

In a flash, Jael is on her feet, knife out toward the woman.

But it's just a girl. A little girl, no more than ten, with a bony stump where her right arm should be.

The girl squeals and darts back into the brush. Jael can still clearly see her shape, darker than the pale sagebrush in the moonlight.

"Who are you?" Jael says. The girl is still close, so Jael doesn't raise her voice.

The silence stretches on and then, "No one."

"What do you want?"

"There's no one here."

The girl's voice is high and tinny but unexpectedly loud, and it takes Jael by surprise. "I'm looking right at you," Jael says.

"Noooo," the girl's voice dips and rises. "This is just a dreeeam. You're still asleeeep."

"Come out here."

"I caaaan't! I'm a dreeeam fairy, and if I get touched by the moooonlight, I'll disappeeeear!" The girl waves her arm slowly while she talks.

Jael lunges for the girl, grabbing at her arm, but she darts nimbly out of reach.

"Hey," the girl says in her normal voice, "that's not a nice thing to do to a dream fairy."

Jael grabs again and this time manages to lock onto the girl's wrist. She drags her out into the clearing where the moonlight is brighter.

"You're not a fairy." The words taste strange in Jael's mouth. "You're a thief and who knows what else, and you're going to tell me what you're doing here." She holds the flat part of her knife against the girl's cheek. The girl stops squirming.

"I'm just looking for food," she says.

A thought occurs to Jael, and she scans the low trees nearby. "Are you alone? Where are your parents?"

The little one-armed girl's voice is quieter. "Yeah, I'm alone."

Jael's eyes snap back to the girl who's looking down at her feet. Her arm is bone thin. Her clothes are ragged: a too-small shirt with the sleeves torn off and a pair of pants that stop well above her ankles.

Still, Jael holds her knife steady. There are plenty of orphans running around in the towns. This one, she reminds herself, was about to steal from her.

"What are you doing here?" Jael asks again.

"I told you, I'm looking for food."

"Not much food out here unless you were planning on stealing from me," Jael says. "But I'm guessing you knew that." She tilts her knife just slightly forward so the edge rests on the girl's cheek.

"I wasn't, I swear," she says. "I just watched real careful how you dug up those roots from beside the trees, and then when you fell asleep I was going to do the same." The girl cuts her wide blue eyes up at Jael. "Which, by the way, you did. You're still asleeeeep."

"You're avoiding the truth. Why are you out in the middle of nowhere?" Jael demands.

"Why are you?" the girl says.

Jael presses the blade as hard as she can without breaking skin, and the girl gulps.

"Fine. I left town a while back because everyone there was mean, and I found this house just through the canyon pass—it even had a well and a garden and everything." The words rush out of her now. "And I lived there and made it cozy and all, and then today I fell asleep out in the Juniper tree, and when I woke up it was all on fire, everything, and the smoke—you could see that smoke from a mile out. I thought I covered my cook fire, but I guess I must have not done a good job. So then I didn't have anywhere to live, so I figured I'd better hit the road, Jack." She mumbles herself to a stop.

Jael swallows against her dry throat. "What happened to your arm?"

"Dunno."

"Of course you know." Jael grabs the front of her shirt, pulling her to her tiptoes. She's hiding something.

"I swear I don't! I was born like this. Radiation or whatever. Same old story."

Jael lets go, and the girl stumbles back a step. Jael looks at her for a moment longer. She closes her eyes and wipes the sweat off her forehead with the back of her fist that's still clenching the knife. "Where are you going now?" she asks finally.

The girl lifts her chin higher, "Oh, that's no problem. I've got an aunt up the road that's going to take me in."

Jael raises an eyebrow.

"You don't have to believe me. It's true. She's waiting for me," the girl says. "I've just got to get there is all."

The moonlight bounces off Jael's knife.

"Hey!" the girl squeals. "Hey, maybe I could stick with you!"

Jael opens her mouth to say no but inhales the heavy scent of smoke from the girl's clothes. "Where does she live?" she asks instead.

"Esper."

Jael curses in her head. They are going the same way. Either let the girl tag along, or say no and she'll just creep behind her anyways. Probably give her away when she is trying to hide.

"Fine," she says after a long moment. The girl smiles wide. She seems not to notice the knife still pointed at her, so Jael raises it higher. "But if you take anything from me, sneak around, talk too loud—anything—don't think I won't hand you over to the first Guard I see."

The girl bobs her head up and down quickly. Jael finally releases her wrist, and the girl rubs her cheek where the knife has been.

"And you still get all your own food."

Another nod.

Jael points to a spare patch of dirt. "Sleep there, where I can see you."

The girl lies down on the hard ground, curling her knees up to her chest and using her arm as a pillow. Jael climbs under her blanket and watches until the girl's eyes start to flutter closed. She gives Jael a small smile before turning over. She's young, maybe nine, with wild strawberry hair that's matted and tangled in a way that mirrors the hard desert wind. After a long while, Jael hears snoring.

Jael lies awake, trying to picture the days ahead. Esper is at least a week of hard walking away. She won't change her pace for the girl. She'll either keep up or she won't, simple as that. And she won't talk to her at all. There'll be no chance of her finding out about the fires or Cole or any of it.

They'll travel in silence, Jael decides.

10

"My name's Agi. What's yours?"

They walked for an hour at most before the little girl speaks, throwing the words out all at once like they've been building pressure inside her.

Jael walks on. After a few moments, the girl skips forward and turns around, walking backwards so she faces Jael.

"I said my name is Agi. What's yours?"

Jael's eyes stay fixed ahead as she answers, "I heard you."

The little girl, Agi apparently, laughs—a jingling sound. "I know you heard me, what else is there to hear out here? It's not like the great crowd of people around us is drowning me out."

She spins once, arm flung out wide, and grins expectantly at Jael, waiting for her to join in on the joke. Jael's eyes pass coolly over the girl before she lifts her chin higher and looks over the top of her head.

Agi lets out a little huff then turns and falls back into step beside Jael. "I was hoping you'd be more fun."

The moments pass by, and Jael realizes Agi's footsteps are falling exactly in rhythm with her own. She glances over and sees Agi staring at her boots. Jael slows her pace slightly, and Agi's steps slow as well. She speeds up, and Agi swings her little arm to match the speed. Jael jerks to a halt then takes several quick steps in a row, and Agi lets out a squeal of delight as she loses the rhythm entirely.

Jael slows her steps into a normal pace. Agi skips to catch up and slips her hand into Jael's. Her tiny fingers are clammy and soft inside Jael's hand.

Jael jerks away and clenches her fist tight.

Agi's steps falter and fall out of rhythm. She starts to lag behind Jael. The little girl kicks a rock across the dusty ground and watches it bounce ahead of her.

"Jael."

Agi purses her lips in the same face Jael's mother used to make when she was in trouble. The adult expression looks funny on the girl's small features. She runs a hand through her strawberry hair and cuts her eyes at Jael.

"Well that's a nice name. Jael." She giggles, a child again. "It sounds kind of like jail, like a prison. Is that how it's spelled? With an 'I'?"

Jael shakes her head. "E."

Agi nods wisely. "That's like my name. People always think it's just the two letters, like it's just spelled A.G." She swings her arm around in circles as she walks. "But it just sounds like that. It's not like it stands for anything." She looks over at Jael. "It's not like I'm Agatha Ginger."

Agi laughs so hard she has to stop walking until she can breathe enough to move on. She is still wearing a broad smile when she jogs up beside Jael. She watches her thin black shoes as she walks, tiptoeing around the scattered buckwheat and creosote bushes.

"Wait!"

Agi stops suddenly, squats on her heels, and peers intently at something on the ground.

Jael stops too. "What's wrong?" she asks, scanning the landscape around them.

"Look at this!" Agi holds up a black rock, patchy with white spots.

"What?"

"Look at it! It's a picture."

Jael kneels down beside her.

"See? It's a little man." Agi sets the rock on the ground and traces the crisscrossing white lines with her finger. "I heard that Indians used to do this to rocks. Like a thousand years ago or something. Did you know that?"

Jael picks it up and rubs her finger over the dips and grooves the white lines have made in the rock.

"Can you read it?" A pause. "Are you an Indian?"

"No."

"I didn't think so. But I had to ask. You're the right color for it, and your hair is really dark, you know." Her eyebrows shoot up seriously as she says the word "really."

Jael stands and brushes the dirt from her knees.

"I wonder why they did that? The rocks, I mean. Do you know what it means?"

"No. I don't." Jael turns from the pavement. "Come on, we're going this way." A narrow dirt road stretches out in front of them into the barren desert.

Agi tucks the rock under the hairy spikes of a prickly pear cactus and trots after her.

* * *

The hours run together, an eternal stretch of scorching sun, dried meat, and Juniper berries. Jael and Agi follow the crumbling road that winds along the gentle hip-curves of the land. The heat makes everything brittle and dry. In the spring, the primroses and ocotillos might have bloomed, but now it's summer, and even the waxy cactus flowers have admitted defeat.

The dirt on the ground bakes under the hot sun and turns easily to dust. The lizards that scurry over it with their hard, chewy skin are always coated in a thin layer of that copper-colored dust.

When the wind starts up, there's nothing to stop it. No trees to block its path. It starts out as just a stirring of the sagebrush. The dry stalks with their paper-shuffling sound echoing the dryness of the whole land.

Then the wind becomes dissatisfied with the sagebrush, and it picks itself up to seek a new home. It slides to the open dirt, swirling it around and around, higher and higher, playing with the little specks of dust until finally it moves back to the line of sagebrush that catches the dirt.

People always say you can't see the wind, that you can only feel it.

But you can see the wind in the desert. You can see it in the dry and cracked dirt, in the waxy leaves of cactus flowers, in the tight little Juniper trees that cling so low to the ground.

And even when it stops, you can see the wind lurking in the distance, watching and waiting. Watching everything dry up. Waiting offstage for its cue: the first sign of moisture.

11

Day three.

"Shhh."

Agi stops walking and closes her eyes.

"Shhhh," she says. "Hear that?"

Jael stands and waits for Agi to finish. The more attention she gets, the longer she drags on. Better to just stand there and wait; the girl will move again in a minute or two. They could both use a break from walking anyway.

Agi drops to the ground, putting her ear right next to a stalk of dried sagebrush. She closes her eyes.

"Can you hear that? That's my favorite sound in the world."

After a few minutes, Jael can't take it anymore. "What are you listening to?"

"Shhhhhh," Agi hisses. "You'll hear."

The wind swirls on them, and Jael can hear the air rubbing against the stalks of sagebrush.

Agi whispers, "I think it sounds like rain. Like how rain would sound if it was dry. Or maybe like something big coming, like a change. Or maybe like things not changing, like things staying the same." She laughs, full and loud. "That doesn't make any sense, does it?"

She looks up at Jael. "What do you think it sounds like?"

Jael listens for a moment. "It sounds like wind."

Agi laughs and closes her eyes again as the wind rushes up through the paper leaves and tickles her cheeks.

Way off in the distance, something breaks the flat line of the horizon. It could be a cactus or a Joshua tree, but it makes Jael uneasy, and it looks like it's moving.

"Come on," she says. "Let's keep going."

They travel until well past sunset, Jael checking over her shoulder every few steps. When they can no longer make out the road in front of them, they stop. Agi whines, but Jael won't let her start a campfire. She's sure now that it was Haskell she saw earlier. The girl falls asleep quickly, but Jael lies awake for hours, listening.

* * *

The dream comes differently this time.

It starts the same, the same awful and wonderful beginning. He's alive again, and she rubs the tips of his fingers again, and he trembles in pain all over again. His eyes open again, and the raw air cuts into Jael as it always does, and she can't breathe, as she never can. The air claws at her lungs until she's sure she'll pass out. She looks into his eyes, hoping for one more moment before the darkness closes in.

And then something deep in his eyes shifts. She finds herself perched on the edge of a deep well, peering down, and the well is hopelessly empty. He's gone. Then she falls in, too, tumbling down and down until it becomes clear there is no bottom. The echo of her scream bounces around her as she falls.

Then somehow the little girl is there. The little one-armed girl. Beside her. Shaking her. And she's awake and sitting up and gasping, and this little girl with one arm is crouched beside her and curling her arm around Jael's shoulders. Jael jerks away from the touch and perches on the edge of the blanket. Her throat is raw.

The girl looks up at the stars for a moment then back over at Jael's huddled form. She starts to sing.

"I can't marry in the summer."

Her singing voice is even brighter than her speaking voice, and it stabs the night sweetly.

"What are you—"

"Shhh. I'll sing and then it will be alright, you'll see." She scoots over to where Jael sits, staying a couple feet away. "Just let me sing and you lay there. It'll work. It's a song my dad sang to my mom. You'll like it, I promise."

She coaxes Jael down and pulls the blanket over her arms. Jael curls onto her side, tucking her knees up to her chest, and watches the little girl lie back and stare intently at the sky.

"I can't marry in the summer.
I can't marry in the winter
'Cause the pretty girl I love
Loves another mister"

She pauses to glance over at Jael, pinching her brow in frustration. "Well, you've got to be looking up at the stars for this part, or else it won't work."

Jael glares at her and settles further into her curled position.

"Oh, don't be stubborn. Go on, lie back. It will work; that's it." They both look up at the pinpoint stars. Agi sings.

"Money, I ain't got any.
I'm a country boy of old."

The strip of hazy light from the Milky Way shines brightest and pulls Jael's focus. Her pulse slows a little as she traces the familiar patterns in the sky and the sweet voice plucks music all around her.

"But the silver stars are my riches,
And the sweet sun is my gold.
And the sweet sun is my gold."

12

Jael wakes to sunburnt cheeks. The little one-armed girl has already packed up camp and stands off in the distance, staring out toward the mid-morning sun. Jael rubs her arms, brushing the dream away like dead skin. She packs up her blanket and goes over to where Agi stands, both of them staring at the unforgiving desert. Jael looks on all sides; no sign of Haskell. They start walking.

Hours later, Agi turns to Jael. "What were you dreaming about?"

Jael swats at a fly buzzing around her head.

"Last night, I mean. When I woke you up. Was it a nightmare?"

"No."

Agi stops at a particularly squat Juniper tree. The little berries she picks are more dust-colored than blue. She tucks them into her pack and jogs to catch back up with Jael.

"Well, whatever it was, it had you all kinds of riled up. You were kicking and shivering all over the place. Was it someone chasing you? I have that nightmare sometimes— where something's chasing me."

"It wasn't a nightmare."

"Well I hope it was, 'cause if that was a happy dream, I don't want to see the unhappy kind." She grins at Jael.

"I didn't say it was happy." Jael looks over at the girl with an expression that means the conversation is over.

"Fine." Agi huffs and walks alongside Jael, quiet for a few minutes. And then—

"It's just that my dad used to sing me that song when I had nightmares. So I figured that's why it worked for you."

Jael pulls her water out of her bag and takes a drink.

"My dad used to say he'd give me a sun gold necklace one day, with silver stars, like in the song."

Jael recaps her water and puts it away.

Agi looks over at Jael. "Are your parents dead?"

Jael doesn't look back. "Yes."

Agi's fingers fiddle with the hem of her shirt.

They walk in silence, watching the desert. When Jael finally speaks, it is hours later.

"What was that song?"

Agi's excited eyes look up at Jael. She opens her mouth wide.

"Diamonds and pearls and ruuubies ain't within my reach. But I'll give you all the love I got, and aaaall the stars I can reach."

Agi giggles as her vowels blend into one another. Her tinny voice pools around them in the desert, filling up all that empty space, and Jael can't help but smile. She's never heard a song like that before. There's something different about it— something honest. It must be old, from the days before.

Jael looks at the girl, wondering how she came across such a song. She assumed Agi has been on her own for a long time. She is tough in the harsh desert, and she hasn't complained once about the relentless pace. But that song—it has been ages since Jael heard anyone sing, and then it was just the hymns that had survived over the decades, thanks to a few devoted religious groups. All the other old songs had dwindled away.

This song is from a time before all that. It's tinged with sadness in the slow melody, but it's overall a hopeful song. Jael doesn't know anyone—other than maybe Cole—who would sing a song like that.

As if reading Jael's thoughts, Agi pipes up again. "You have to promise not to sing it to anyone, okay? Not unless they really need it. My dad would sing it to me, but he made me promise to keep it a secret unless somebody really needed it." She looks down at her feet, avoiding Jael's eyes. "It's more special that way, he said. He heard it from his dad's dad's dad's dad." She counts on her fingers until she gets to four. "From way back before the fallout."

Agi's voice takes on a formal air, and Jael can tell she's started reciting a story she's heard many times. "Have you ever heard of Miss Ippi?" she asks. She moves on without waiting for a response. "Miss Ippi was a place way back before the fallout, way far away from here, and a long time ago our family lived there—" She shoots a look at Jael. "My family, I mean. That's just how my dad would say it. He would say 'our' because he was talking to me. But I meant to say 'my'." She seems satisfied and brushes her hair over her shoulder before resuming her wispy, formal tone.

"Anyways, my family lived in Miss Ippi, and it was down south near the ocean. They got so much rain down there that the trees shot up everywhere. And not Juniper trees—big ones, every one of them taller than a building and just as green as you can imagine. And they were everywhere. So many of them that you couldn't hardly walk three steps in any direction without stepping on a root.

"And my dad's dad's dad's dad played this thing called a banjo, which was sort of like a mix between a guitar and a drum. Though I don't really know what that means. And one day, he met this girl. Boy, she was beautiful. Hair as red as a strawberry and skin as white as a cloud, and—snap!—just like that he was in love. But he was poor and she was rich, so he didn't think it would work out much between them. But still, he loved her, and so he came every day to the bench where she liked to sit and look at the trees, and the leaves, and the shade. He went there every day and played his banjo and sang that song to her, and every day she fell more and more in love with him.

"Then one day, it was the first day of spring, he picked a handful of flowers—there were flowers all over the place there—and he twisted two of them together and gave it to her as an engagement ring and said—"

Agi breaks off when she realizes Jael stopped walking. Jael stands there, mouth slightly open, staring toward Agi without really looking at her.

"That's what he did." She talks quietly, and Agi has to take a few steps to hear her. "He found some bright pink flowers and made them into a ring and put it on my finger and told me he wanted to be with me." She rubs her empty ring finger absently. "I've got no clue how he found those flowers. They were so bright…"

"You have a husband? That's so romantic!" Agi says excitedly.

Jael says nothing, still staring at her hand.

"Is that why you're going to Esper? He's waiting there?" Agi practically bounces on her feet.

"No."

Agi slows her bouncing. After a moment, she asks, "Well, where is he?"

Jael says, "Nowhere," while thinking *everywhere*.

For once, Agi stays quiet. Jael sits down heavily on the dirt, the memory so sharp and unexpected that her legs are weak. Agi sits down several feet away and pulls her knees to her chest with her arm. The wind swirls around them, and Jael shuts her eyes to keep out the dust. When she opens them again minutes later, Agi has taken Juniper berries and old bread out of her bag and is settled down to eat.

Jael feels shaky. She didn't mean to tell the girl all that. Had she said his name? She didn't think so. How did she pull that out of her? It was just the coincidence of the stories, she tells herself. She's just a girl. She'll forget about it; she'll move on. She'll find some new obsession—a rock or a lizard or a weed—and she'll forget all about this.

Practically on cue, Agi pipes up. "What is that?"

Jael looks around. "What?"

"That." Agi points at her. "That necklace."

The round diamond catches the light until Jael pinches it between her fingers. She tucks the necklace back under her shirt. "Nothing," she says and stands up. "Come on. We're losing the light."

As Agi shoves the rest of the berries into her mouth, Jael starts to calculate. There are a hundred options. Her heart beats faster and her worry fades away as she compiles a list of the hundred ways she could, in a moment's notice, be rid of the girl.

13

"Hey, there's something up there!" Agi breaks the silence just before sunset.

Jael doesn't need to look up. She knows where they are. She knows that the creosote is growing thicker, that off to the right there is a line of cottonwoods and behind them a wash, and that just ahead is a vegetable farm owned by a nice old couple called Mr. and Mrs. Bower. She could walk the rest of the way blindfolded.

At the thought of it, Jael's chest tightens. She pictures old Mrs. Bower opening her arms to Jael, looking at her in that silent, maternal way of hers.

Agi squints into the early evening sun. "I think it's a farm."

Jael puts her bag on the ground and starts to pull out food: a hard crust of bread, an almost-bad apple, and a small tear of dried meat.

"What are you doing?" Agi asks.

"What does it look like?" Jael spreads her blanket on the ground and crosses her legs, settling into her meal.

"You are *not* serious." Agi's mouth gapes open.

Jael simply tears the jerky with her teeth and chews slowly.

"But we're so close! We could make it there tonight. They probably have food and water and beds and everything!"

"No one's stopping you."

Agi's head swivels back and forth between Jael and the farm. "You're nuts, you know that?" she says and plops down on the ground, pouting with her chin in her hands. "Crazy as a racoon in heat."

Jael is so startled, she laughs. She looks at Agi. "What did you just say?"

The corners of Agi's mouth turn up slowly from their pout. Her blue eyes shine.

"Crazy as a what?" Jael presses.

"As a racoon in heat?" she says sheepishly. She rushes on, "It's something my dad used to say. If I was acting out, he'd pinch my ear and say, 'Girl, you are actin' crazy as a racoon in heat.' Then he'd whack me on the butt, and I'd have to sit still with my hand in my lap until he decided to let me up."

Jael laughs even harder until her stomach cramps and the red sunset turns watery in her vision.

Agi giggles as she spreads out her blanket for sleep. "You really are crazy, you know."

The light is dim. The moon already high in the sky is becoming brighter by the minute, a silver dollar hung above their heads.

The girl falls quickly into sleep, her arm tucked under her as a pillow. Jael faces the town. A few buildings sit low in the distance, square lines and edges jutting out from the horizon. Jael traces each one with her eyes. The tallest one is the Bower's, though even it is barely two stories high—a big, dusty red farmhouse. There's a cluster of one-room worker's shacks off to the left and an old, broken-down wind turbine behind them. Then, farther left, the landscape smooths out. For miles, nothing breaks the flat line of the horizon. It looks as though, if you were to walk all the way there, you would reach that line and simply fall off. For a very long time, Jael sits and stares at the edge of the world.

When the sky is finally without any hint of red, Jael stands up. She tucks her knife into her boot and the matchbook into the back pocket of her jeans. The full moon lights up the sagebrush before her and turns it a whiter shade of gray than it was under the sun. She shifts her weight, and her leather boots sigh into fine red sand.

While Agi sleeps, Jael starts walking.

14

The sand turns to crust. Her boots crunch the ground now, and her throat is rough and stinging from the chilled air, but at least there is no sun to beat her down. The moon rises higher and then starts to sink fast like a ball thrown up into the air only to hover up high and fall again with greater speed.

Finally, Jael stands on the edge of the field. The crop— corn this time—is struggling to grow. The stalks are shorter than they should be by this time of year. There hasn't been much rain. It will be a small return for a year's worth of hard work.

From the middle of the field, Jael hears something. She can't quite make out the words, but she knows the voice. The laugh. The lilting rhythm of rise and fall in that deep tone. The base of her skull throbs with the beginnings of a headache.

She runs to him.

The sound is always just slightly out of her reach, just barely on the edge.

Him: "What's your name?"

Her: "You know my name."

Bits of conversation float in the air. She runs frantically, trying to grab each sound, each syllable, before it floats away.

Him: "But you don't know mine."

Her: "It's a small town. Word gets around."

A corn stalk grabs her ankle, and she trips, scraping her hands and knees on the rough dirt. She claws her way forward.

Him: "So there's no mystery left?"

Her: "Nope. None."

Him: "I bet you don't know what I'm thinking right now."

She crawls farther. Just a few more feet and he'll be there, she's sure of it. She'll be able to see him. Touch him. Finally.

Her: "Probably not."

Him: "You look like a warrior."

Her: Laughter.

Him: "I'm serious. The honey-colored skin. The black hair blowing wildly in the wind. Like a great, powerful warrior from centuries ago."

Her: More laughter. "What a line."

The matchbook is too light in her hands. She clutches her numb fingers around it, trying desperately to keep it from falling from her hand.

"Jael."

His voice is in her ear, so close that she spins around.

But he's not there. The black sky and the white moon and the empty field... and nothing else. She is alone. She knows what she has to do.

She strikes a match.

15

The dry corn stalks are scratchy on Agi's skin, but she stays crouched low, out of the light from their campfire. She peers into the field.

For a while, she watches Jael run wildly through the rows of corn. Then Jael disappears from view. Agi can hear crying.

The girl crouches even lower to the ground, pinned down by the broken sounds coming from Jael. She's never heard crying like that. And muttering too, like she's talking to someone, but there's no one there. For some reason, an image of the purple flower ring pops into Agi's head.

All at once, the sun breaks the horizon and turns the sky orange.

No.

It's something else.

The light is too irregular. It ebbs and flows like an orange ocean. It shoots up high in one great burst, and Agi smells smoke.

Fire.

The world turns sideways and Agi falls. The whole field is on fire, faster than she would have thought possible. She pictures the little matchbook Jael always slips into her back pocket in the mornings.

Then she sees Jael coughing and stumbling away from the field, back towards their camp.

The thought occurs to Agi that she could just run away. She could pound on the door of the nearest building and scream for help. But the broken sobbing sounds echo in Agi's head, though she can no longer hear them. She remembers the way Jael shook in her sleep.

All of these thoughts flash through her head in a matter of seconds, and then she sprints back to the campsite. She focuses on calming her breathing enough to look like she's sleeping soundly by the time Jael gets back.

16

Haskell is standing on top of a mesa, scanning the land for campfires. So far nothing. Which either means Jael is nowhere nearby, or her fire is too small to be seen from here. Or she's too smart to light a fire in the first place. Haskell curses under his breath and tosses his hair back.

He lost her track yesterday afternoon, but she couldn't have gone that far. He spent most of the afternoon climbing to the top of the mesa, just to catch a glimpse of a nonexistent campfire. This girl was proving a bigger challenge that he'd expected.

Haskell takes a deep breath and looks up at the stars. He likes challenges. He likes the chase, the hunt, the kill. It's how he's always survived. Besides, this one is worth it. That necklace will fetch a price high enough for him to settle down anywhere he wants. He just has to get it from her.

Something flickers in the bottom of his vision and his eyes snap to it.

A fire. Finally.

But there's too much smoke for a campfire. The flames shoot up way too high. A wildfire, then? Some sort of accident?

Or perhaps one that's not an accident at all.

Haskell quickly throws his blanket and water jug into his bag and starts the long, winding trail down the back of the mesa. If he hurries, he can be there by morning.

17

Jael wakes Agi before dawn. Agi shuffles along, half-asleep. They give the field a wide berth. The workers finally got the fire under control sometime after midnight, but the scent of smoke still lingers in the air. The girl must be really groggy from sleep, because she doesn't seem to notice. If they can just get past the field before morning... Jael knows Old Mr. Bower; he will have already called a Guard to catch whoever started the fire. The farther they can get, the better.

Jael's gut twists as she thinks about all those crops gone. She knows exactly what that will mean for the Bowers and all their workers. It will be a miracle if they bounce back.

But still, it had to happen. She didn't have a choice, Jael tells herself.

When the sun finally rises, Jael is almost convinced they are in the clear. The road is open behind them, and they are past the trees. She will be able to see anyone coming from a mile off. But then, the converse of that is also true.

By the end of the day, the landscape starts to change. The sweeping desert grasslands are still there, but in the distance the gradually sloping mesas are replaced with towering piles of rocks rising up and up in skinny spires. In one section of the horizon, the rocks have been carved into flat triangles, all leaning against each other like huge mountain set pieces for the stage.

With the sun setting fast, they camp out in the open grass for one more night. Tomorrow they'll be at the rocks with plenty of places to hide. A lizard stuffs its nose into Jael's bag, sniffing out the dried meat and fruit. It has three legs and a short, stubby tail. Jael swats it away and ties the bag up tighter to keep the lizard from coming back.

Agi clutches her knees to her chest as Jael hunts and eventually catches a white-tailed jackrabbit. Her eyes follow Jael as she strikes a match to get the campfire going. They eat in silence, and the girl is still sitting in the same spot, staring up at the stars now, when Jael drifts slowly off to sleep.

* * *

Just before they reach the rocks, Jael feels the tell-tale insects buzzing around her neck. There's an abandoned gas station a ways off, and they veer off track, feeling the weightlessness of their empty water jugs banging against their hips.

The gas station bears the signs of having been turned into a trading post at some point. After the fallout, spots like this popped up all over the place, but this one clearly wasn't worth the effort of maintaining. The windows are shattered, the pump hoses gone. Jael peers inside as they pass, and the little store is completely empty.

The good news is the water tank in the back. It's huge, wider than a bathtub, almost like a pool. Jael climbs up and cranks open the lid.

"Phew!" she says, pulling her head back quickly. "That water is way too stale to drink."

Before Jael has a chance to protest, Agi has climbed up and jumped in feet first. She lands with a plunk on the bottom. She giggles as the water tickles her armpits. "It looked deeper." She looks at Jael. "Aren't you coming in?" she asks.

"No." Jael climbs back down.

Agi clumsily climbs out. Her footsteps are sloppish from her soggy shoes on the dirt.

Jael feels something wet sprinkle across the back of her neck. She turns around to see Agi whipping her wet hair back and forth. Another spray of water catches Jael right across her face.

"Stop it," she says.

Agi flops her hand on her hip. "You've got to get in. The water is just perfect, and if you don't get in, we will both regret it; you because you missed out on this nice cool water, and me because I'll have to keep smelling you like that. Forever." Agi pinches her nose and stares at Jael who stares back coolly. Agi taps her foot rapidly on the ground.

Jael bends down to unlace her boots, and Agi squeals and runs full-force back into the tank. She jumps in with a huge splash.

Jael finishes stripping off her boots, and by the time she reaches the top of the ladder, Agi is up and bouncing about again. Jael sits on the edge of the tank and lets her feet dangle into the water. She slips into the tank and sits on the bottom, folding her legs beneath her. The water plays against her brown collarbone in a soft way that brings her against her will to thoughts of him. On their first night together, Cole ran his thumb across the length of her collarbone just like that. He looked at her with steady, awed eyes that held no secret or hidden message—just an open and obvious wonder at the beauty of a sloping curve of bone under a tight stretch of skin.

Agi's splashing calls Jael back, and she opens her eyes wondering when she closed them. She turns her head to see Agi still playing on the other side of the tank. Jael pushes herself out to the middle and flips onto her back. The water bobs gently from Agi's movements.

Floating on her back, Jael lets go of each muscle in turn until her whole body is balanced on the border between water and sky. Jael's mind goes back to something Agi said a few minutes before. It struck as an odd note, and now she pulls out the words, spreads them apart from one another, and focuses on the one that doesn't fit.

Forever.

The word is spiky in Jael's brain. She can't find a place to put it. She puts it in her present, and it cuts against images of fire on the desert. She tries throwing it in with her future, but that section of her brain only has slots for a few words, and those are already filled with things like "tonight" and "tomorrow" and "water." Finally, she settles on tucking it in with her past, an area reserved for things that have failed. There are so many jagged edges in that section already, what's one more going to matter? She lets her feet fall to the bottom of the tank. Wading over to the edge again, she climbs out with water dripping down from her body and making a puddle beneath her.

In a few minutes she will be mostly dry, and in a few minutes more she will call Agi out of the water. In an hour or two, they will have set up camp and cooked dinner, and in another hour, they will be fed and sleeping. Then the sun will rise and they will walk some more. Eventually they will reach Esper. Jael lies back on the ground, closes her eyes to the glaring sun, and enjoys the feeling of seeing her future laid out before her.

18

It takes another long, hard day of walking, but they finally reach the massive rock structures in the late afternoon. They could go around them, but the quickest way to Nettletown, and past that, Esper, is to go straight through them.

Agi pulls ahead to take the lead, and Jael lets her.

In an unexpected curve, they find themselves below a massive arch in the rocks. It towers twenty feet above their heads or higher. To one side of the arch, a mound of small, smooth boulders sits almost level with the top of the arch. Agi runs to stand below the arch, craning her neck back to look at it.

"I wonder how this happens," Agi says, running her hand along the smooth base of the arch.

Jael doesn't say anything.

"How an arch like this happens," Agi clarifies.

"Water," Jael says, almost to herself.

Agi looks at Jael, scathingly. "We're in the desert."

"It comes up from underneath. Water from deep down seeps up and wears away at the rock from the bottom, making an arch." Jael points at the bottom, showing the layered lines of rock at the base.

Agi's hard look softens a little, and her eyebrows rise. "Is that the truth?"

Jael nods.

"How do you know?"

"Just do."

Jael walks to the side, drops her bag on the ground, and climbs the pile of rocks until she is high enough to jump over to the top of the arch. Agi watches from below with wide eyes. She calls up something, but Jael can't make out the words. When Jael doesn't answer, Agi huffs and stomps away through a gap in the sandstone.

Jael inches out to the center of the arch. She can feel a soft breeze, and the heat is, for the moment, bearable. The wind curls around her jaw and plucks a few strands of thick black hair loose from their knot. She lets the wind juggle her hair, yanking it back and forth across her face.

In certain moments, the insistent fingers of the wind feel just the same as his hands running through her hair. He always said her hair was what made him fall in love. The way she let it fly loose while she was working, impractical as it was.

Jael undoes the knot and surrenders it to the wind. Through a blur of hair she sees the hills in the distance, and though she can't see it, she knows Nettletown sits in the valley just beyond. Somewhere past that waits Esper.

Just a few more days.

Jael turns slowly and scans the opposite horizon, but there's not a soul in sight, making Jael even uneasier. The Bower farm was over the line. There will be someone looking for her now, if there wasn't already. A few days. That's all. She'll be somewhere new—somewhere with no memories, no past. Then she'll have it under control. She'll be able to start over. To breathe.

To her left, she hears a sudden clink of rocks tumbling down. A hand clutches the top of the smooth boulder, and a man climbs into view.

Haskell's face is purple from over-exertion. His long hair sticks sweaty to his forehead. When he finally stands atop the rocks, he holds a hand out to Jael to help him across the gap. When she just stares at him, he lets his hand fall.

"Well hello to you, too," he mutters. Bending his legs, he propels himself across the gap and lands awkwardly on his knees at Jael's feet. He clings to either side of the arch, panting. "That was a lot farther than it looked."

After a few shaky breaths, he gets to his feet. He looks down and whistles between his teeth. "Don't know how you're standing so calm up here."

"What are you doing?" Jael asks.

"At the moment? I'm trying not to collapse into a puddle of fear." He pulls his gaze away from the ground to look at her. His eyes snag on her hand. She realizes she's fiddling with the pendant around her neck, pulling it back and forth on its chain. She tucks it under her shirt.

She tries again. "What do you want?"

"I told you before, I just want to make sure you're okay. Cole being my brother and all. I've been following since you ran off; let me just tell you, you are not an easy girl to keep up with."

Jael squints at him. "You've been following me."

He smiles. "That's right." When Jael doesn't say anything, he pushes his hair back and crosses his arms. "Where are you running to, anyways?" he asks.

"I'm not running anywhere."

He quirks an eyebrow. "It's fine, I get it. A new start and all that. You thinkin' Molb? Esper?"

Jael must have reacted somehow, because he grins and nods. "Ahh, Esper," he says. "Nice town, I hear."

"Hey!" Agi's high-pitched voice is louder than Jael would have believed possible. "Hey, you! You leave her alone!"

Haskell looks down at the girl, and his lips quirk up into a smile. "Well, now this is a surprise." He looks over at Jael but speaks loud enough for Agi to hear. "I didn't know you had a girl."

"She's not my daughter—"

"She's not my mom—"

They speak loudly and simultaneously. Their eyes lock until Haskell's chuckle breaks the tension.

"Whatever you say." He shakes his head. "Listen," he calls to Agi, "I just want to have a talk with your... not mom. So just walk out that way 'til you count to a hundred and then walk back. We'll be done by then."

Agi purses her lips. Haskell shoos her away with his hands.

Agi puts her hand on her hip and yells up at him. "Maybe she doesn't want to talk to you!"

Haskell looks over at Jael and raises an eyebrow. "You know this girl?"

Jael shrugs.

"Listen," he calls, "I don't know who you are, but me and Jael go way back. We're fine here." He wraps an arm around Jael's shoulders, and she stiffens.

When Agi still doesn't move, his arm curls a little bit tighter around Jael's neck.

"Just go," Jael calls down.

Agi's eyes search Jael's face. "You want to talk to him?"

"You need to keep your nose out of my business," Jael says. "I don't want you here."

Agi's mouth drops open. She spins around and stomps away, pausing once to throw Jael a murderous look over her shoulder.

"Charming." Haskell watches her huff away. "Friend of yours?"

Jael shoves Haskell's arm off of her and backs as far away from him as she can on the narrow arch.

"You need to stop following me," she demands.

"But we're family now." His mouth is a straight line, but his eyes laugh at her.

She ignores his question. "What. Do. You. Want?" Her jaw is tight.

He takes a breath. "Fine. I need something of Cole's. Well, it wasn't really his, but he had it, and I want it back."

Jael holds out her empty hands. "I didn't keep anything of his."

"Let's not play this game, Jael." He takes a step forward. "We both know I just saw it."

Jael doesn't move.

"It was our mother's necklace. She always said she was going to give it to me someday. Cole knew that, but he stole it anyway after she died and ran away before she was cold under the ground."

"I don't believe that. And I can't give it to you."

His eyes snap up to her face. "It's mine." He sounds suddenly like a kid, whining.

Jael just stares at him.

"I'm not leaving without that necklace." He takes another step toward her. Jael starts to step back but feels the sloping edge of the arch under her feet. She looks down, and the ground zooms away from her. She turns back to him.

"Why do you want it so bad?" The wind flares up again, tugging on the back of Jael's shirt.

"It's part of my family."

"It's worth a lot of money, you mean."

Haskell's eyebrows knit together. "It's mine, no matter the reason. It was never Cole's in the first place." He shuffles forward another step, legs shaking from the height. "He stole it, and I am taking it back."

His eyes no longer look anything like Cole's. They are hard and cold, and up close Jael can see flecks of gold.

She pulls the chain over her head and coils it in her hand. Haskell smiles, surprised. He reaches out to her, and she hurls the necklace as hard as she can. It glitters in the air and then arches over a nearby boulder and is gone from sight.

His mouth hangs open, his arm still poised in the air. He turns to Jael, fists clenching.

"Do you even know what you just did?" He grabs Jael by the wrist. He twists her arm sharply to the right, and she gasps, bending with it to keep the bone from snapping. Her face is now turned to the ground, which looks, if possible, even further away than the last time. Rocks clutter the space below her.

Haskell jerks his head to clear the hair from his eyes. "You're going to go find it for me." He twists harder, and she drops to her knees. "Right?"

Jael can feel the bone in her wrist squeaking as it threatens to break. Her eyes are wet as she nods once.

He drops her hand, and she pulls it to her chest, cradling it with her other arm. She squints up at him. The sun sits just behind his head, blocking his face from view. All she can see are his stiff shoulders heaving up and down as he tries to catch his breath.

In one quick movement, she kicks her foot out, throwing his legs from under him. For a moment, he's suspended and his arms flail wildly. Then, he hits the rock hard with his shoulder before sliding off the edge of the arch. Jael hears the thump before she looks down.

His arm is bent at a wrong angle, and the blood snakes a curved line in the ground, trailing out from his elbow.

Jael jumps the gap, rocks scratching her hands as she grabs all the wrong holds on her way down. She tries not to look at him, but her eyes are drawn just long enough to tell his chest is rising and falling slowly.

She grabs her bag and runs around to the other side of the boulder, scanning the ground frantically for any sign of the necklace.

Nothing.

She climbs a nearby boulder and peers down at the creosote bushes. She curses under her breath. It shouldn't be this hard to find.

Back on the ground, she rifles through each bush, ignoring the way the papery plants scratch her skin.

She hears something behind her and bolts up, fists raised, ready to fight.

It's the girl.

Agi stops in her tracks and raises her hand in the air. "Jeeze, relax. It's just me." Something glitters between her fingers.

Jael's eyes snap to the necklace, dangling from the girl's hand. "Give that back," she demands.

Agi pulls her arm to her chest. "You threw it away. Finders keepers."

In a flash, Jael is to the girl, wrestling the necklace away from the girl's skinny arm.

"Ow!" Agi cries. "Stop it!"

Jael finally wrenches the necklace free. She slumps to the ground, breathing deeply. The nausea fades when she puts her head between her knees.

Agi watches Jael for a minute, her eyes watery. Jael wipes the sweat from her forehead with the back of her hand and looks around at the gray rocks and gray desert plants. The sky overhead is too bright, and everything is too hot. The wind is still.

"Who was that guy?"

Jael stands and places the chain over her head. She tucks the dusty diamond under her shirt. She'll clean it later.

"What did he want?" Agi is squinting her eyes at her. Her foot is tapping again.

"We're leaving," Jael says.

Agi's foot stills. "Wait. What happened? Is he gone?"

"I said we're leaving." Jael turns to go.

Agi drops her bag on the ground with a thud and plops down beside it. "I'm not going anywhere 'til you tell me what's going on."

Jael runs her hand through her hair and ties it back into a knot. "It doesn't matter. Can we please just go?"

Agi pointedly ignores her, plucking wiry stalks of sagebrush from the ground angrily.

"Alright, fine," Jael says. "I'm leaving."

"Hey, wait!"

Agi has to run to keep up with Jael's long strides.

19

Jael's thoughts fly apart as they walk in silence toward the next town. She's been too open around the girl; that's going to have to stop now.

Memories push in at her, clouding her vision. She tries to hold them back, but it's like trying to keep a wave off the shore. She falls a few steps behind Agi and lets the memory crash.

She's back several years, back to when she and Cole were first married. She's standing by the fire, stirring a pot of soup, when Cole comes running up. He bounds over to her, picks her up by the waist, and swings her around once in the center of the small room. He plops her down and starts clapping his hands, like he always did when he was excited. She grabs hold of his hands to keep them still and looks at him expectantly. He grins.

"Well?" she asks.

His voice is surprisingly steady. With a teasing secret in his eyes, he says, "I've got your birthday present."

Of all the things she was expecting him to say, this was not one of them. She blinks. "My birthday was last month. You already gave me something." She points to a delicate cup on the table patterned with blue trees.

He grins and shakes his head. "This is for next year."

She laughs, making his grin widen even further. "That's not fair," she says. "You can't tell me about it and make me wait a whole year."

"Sure, I can. It's my present, isn't it?"

"I thought it was mine."

"Well until I give it to you, it's mine. Actually it's been mine for a long time, and my mom's before that, but, anyways, it's definitely not yours."

She crosses her arms and turns away. "You're such a tease." She goes back to the soup, but before she gets there he comes up behind her and pulls her close, his arms wrapped across her stomach.

"You'll just have to be patient." He brushes her coarse hair over her shoulder and kisses the back of her neck, a feather against her brown skin. "You're going to love it, Jay."

Jael trips over a Juniper root and falls on the ground, her hands swinging up at the last moment to save her head from crashing into a rock. Agi runs to her, touching Jael lightly on the back.

"Jael, are you okay?"

She pushes Agi's hand off and stands up without brushing the dirt from her pants. Her wrist throbs. She starts walking.

"Jael?"

"I fell, Agi. I'm fine."

The horizon of blue sky and red earth is blurry as she tries to ignore the pain radiating up from her wrist. She can hear Agi when she shuffles her feet, following.

It doesn't matter, she tells herself. It's time. It's past time. It's been too long as it is.

Her thoughts unravel as soon as she puts them together, and her mind jumps back to him.

After he got sick, she found a small box wrapped in brown paper and stuffed under a heavy winter blanket. Cole was finally asleep between bouts of coughing, so she stepped outside where the rustling paper wouldn't wake him. The necklace sat inside the box, wrapped around a stick to keep from tangling.

Jael remembers thinking it was the most beautiful thing she'd ever seen. So small and delicate. So unlike her personality, but that was probably what she liked most about it. It was from the world before, and it had no place in the harsh desert. She liked that.

She meant to thank him for it, but the next day he was in so much pain she spent the whole day boiling water so the steam would ease his broken lungs.

20

Jael hears the wagon before she sees it. A low rattling from the loose boards and uneven ground. Agi hears it a moment later and turns to look. From the west, an old hay wagon, the type that used to be hitched up behind a tractor, rolls toward them. It's been modified: a seat bolted onto the front and a hitch that now connects to the back of a horse.

Agi turns quickly to Jael. "We're going to ask for a ride, right?"

Jael squints over her shoulder at the wagon. It's drawing steadily closer. "We don't know them."

Agi's mouth drops open. "So what?"

"Why would they give us a ride?"

"Umm, because they're human?"

Before Jael can say anything, Agi is off and running. Jael curses under her breath and runs after her. As she gets closer, Jael can see the cart is empty but for the driver perched on the front seat, an old man with a wild shock of white hair that sticks up impossibly high on his head.

Agi reaches him before Jael, and the man pulls up on the horse's reins. "Woahh," he calls. "Easy now." The horse jerks its head up before it slows to a stop and sniffs Agi curiously. She giggles.

"Don't mind Sugarnose. She's just got a sweet tooth. Sniffin' your bag for somethin' to eat."

"She's not going to find anything," Agi laughs. "Unless she likes Juniper berries."

"Can't say as she does."

Jael slows down when she gets close and comes to a stop a few yards back.

"Why'd you name her Sugarnose?" Agi asks.

"'Cause it's all she'd eat when I first got her. Took a month to train her to eat anything else."

Agi walks around to the back of the wagon. "Why are you driving an empty cart?" she calls.

"Didn't start out empty," the man calls back. "I just came from Follind and sold every bit of corn I had with me."

Agi skips back to the front of the wagon and pets Sugarnose. "Where you goin' now?" she asks.

"Home," he says. "Nettletown. Big city an hour or so over the hill." He points straight ahead.

Agi spins around and walks right up to him.

"Hey, that's the way we're going!" She runs her hand along the wood of the cart and looks back up at him. "My name's Agi. What's yours?"

"Cloyd."

Agi grins and holds out her left hand to him. Cloyd smiles and shakes it.

He looks to Jael. "And you must be mom?"

"No," Agi says quickly. "My mom died when I was born. This is just Jael. We're traveling together."

Cloyd's eyes dim as he looks back at Agi. "Oh, I'm sorry to hear about your mom," he says.

"Oh, it's fine. Practically all the kids I know are orphans, so it's no big deal." She smiles. "Besides, I'm pretty smart on the streets. I can run circles around all those other kids."

"I bet you can," Cloyd says.

"One time, I even traded this lady a bottle of rat poison, and she gave me a week's worth of dried meat. But it was just water from the creek, mixed with a little cactus juice!"

The old man chuckles.

Jael walks forward and steps between Agi and the old man. "So can you give us a lift?" she asks. "We can pay."

Agi rolls her eyes. "Way to be polite, Jael."

Cloyd chuckles. "You're welcome to ride, but I won't hear of payment." He shakes his head and pushes his hair down absentmindedly. It sticks right back up. "We're going there anyways, and Sugarnose here could use the exercise."

Jael holds his eyes, unsmiling. "We'll pay."

After a moment, Cloyd nods slowly. "If you say so," he says.

* * *

It's a bumpy ride. Sugarnose walks in a wandering, zigzagging line, and Cloyd does little to correct her. Jael and Agi sit in the far back of the wagon. Agi's eyes are bright, jumping from object to object. It's the same desert they've been walking through for days, but Agi looks around like she's never seen anything so wonderful. Jael shuts her eyes against the glaring sun.

"Who's that guy?"

Jael jerks awake, unable to remember falling asleep. She twists around, searching for a figure in the desert.

"What guy?" she asks when she doesn't see anyone.

Agi is lying on her back, watching the clouds. "That guy. The one you were talking to up on the arch."

Jael rubs the back of her neck. "No one."

"I don't like him." Agi lifts her arm in the air above her and waves it around, feeling the wind.

Jael slumps down to rest her head on the side of the cart.

"How do you know him?" Agi asks.

"I don't."

Agi sits up and faces Jael. "So what did he want then?"

"He was trying to steal from me. Can you let it go?" Jael shifts to the corner of the wagon, farther away from the girl.

Agi scoots closer. She's sitting on her knees, almost touching Jael.

"He was gonna steal something? Was it your necklace? Is that why you threw it away? How did you get away?"

"I pushed him off." Jael curls her legs in to her chest.

The girl's eyes go wide as saucers. "Off the arch?! Did he die?"

"No, Agi. He didn't die." Jael looks away.

The wagon wheel hits a rock, and they sway violently to the right. "Hold on to what you got!" Cloyd yells from the front.

"Is he gonna follow us?" Agi asks Jael once the cart has righted itself.

"No," Jael says sternly.

Agi raises an eyebrow. "How do you know?"

"He's not." Jael looks over her shoulder. They're coming around the side of a mesa, and she can start to make out buildings, low and squat against the sky.

Agi is still looking at Jael. "Why didn't you just give him the necklace?"

"Because it's mine." More buildings now. Closer.

"Did Cole give it to you?"

Jael whips around. "What did you say?"

Agi picks at the wagon with her fingernail. "I don't know… I just figured maybe that's why it meant so much to you. You're always fiddling with it and stuff. I don't know."

Jael's heart pounds in her lungs, making it hard to breathe. Her hands curl into fists. "How do you know about him?"

"You said something about him. After you had that nightmare and we were talking about the flower ring and…" She shrugs her shoulder. "Plus you talk in your sleep."

All Jael can remember of her dreams is hot, blue fire. And his face. "Those are just nightmares. They're not real." She's not sure if she's saying this to herself or to the girl.

Agi nods. "I know."

Jael tries to shake the dreams from her head. She looks around again. She can make out details on the buildings now. It's a big town, much bigger than her own, with buildings pushed right up against each other, covered in chipped advertisements for long-since forgotten things like Coca-Cola and injury lawyers. Jael wonders how there's enough food and water to support a town this big. The wagon pulls sharply to the left as the horse darts off after a lizard. Jael catches herself with her hands, and her wrist throbs again.

"Can you get control of your horse?" she yells at Cloyd.

"No can do." The old man's hand is over his eyes, blocking out the sun. The reins are tied to a pole on the cart. "Sugarnose has got a mind of her own." He nods emphatically, agreeing with himself.

The horse has now stopped to sniff a cactus. Jael takes a deep breath.

"But he was real, wasn't he? Cole?" Agi's brow is furrowed. "Not just a nightmare, I mean. Did he die?"

Bile rises up hot in Jael's throat. She pulls her matchbook from her back pocket and rubs her thumb across the black gritty strip. "We're not talking about this."

Agi sits up straighter. "Was it an accident? Did he get sick?"

"I said we're not talking about this!" Her voice is high, hysterical, and the horse neighs and rears back on its hind legs. Cloyd grabs the reins and hurries to calm her, speaking in a slow, soothing voice.

Jael squeezes her eyes shut, but the wood of the wagon fills her vision anyway. It would catch so easy. Her thumb and forefinger pinch the matchbook hard enough that her skin turns white.

"What's going on back there?" the old man calls to them once the horse is calmed. "Are you both fools? Scaring a horse like that… Keep it down, would ya?"

Jael can barely hear him over the pounding in her head. She clenches her jaw, telling herself to hold it together just a little longer, just until they get to the city, just until she can get away. The cart starts moving again.

She glances up, and the girl is still watching her. Jael yanks the chain over her head and puts it in her pocket.

Agi opens her mouth, but Jael cuts her off. "It's nothing," she says. "I kept it for the money. I'm selling it as soon as we get into the city."

Agi just watches her as Sugarnose jerks them slowly toward Nettletown.

21

Haskell wakes to the feeling of a tongue on his cheek. He yelps and something small and furry scurries away into the night.

He sits up and quickly takes stock of the pains in his body. His arm, first and foremost. It's bent horribly the wrong way, and he takes quick sharp breaths around the stabbing pain. That damn girl. He uses his good hand to feel his face, and it comes away sticky with blood. His cheek is all scratched up from the rocks, probably scarred.

He slowly pulls himself to his feet, groaning loudly with the effort. He looks up at the moon. It's been at least five hours since the fight. A five hour head-start—that's what he's up against now. He kicks at a rock. He'll never catch her now.

Esper.

That's what she'd said, right? Well, she hadn't outright said it. But he knew. The way she tightened her jaw—that was her tell. She was heading to Esper, he'd bet his life on it.

He laughs grimly as he realizes that is exactly what he is doing—betting his life on it. This arm won't heal on its own. He'll need a Healer, and they don't come cheap.

He clenches his good hand into a fist and starts walking. In the moonlight, it's too dark to see her trail, but it doesn't matter. He doesn't need it anymore.

He knows exactly where to find her.

22

It's market day in Nettletown, and no one notices the ragged girl and tired young woman wandering through the streets. The buildings are old, built from the leftovers of a dead industrial society. Metal frames that shine red from rust cling to crumbling walls. But still, life flows on. They pass a grocer, a butcher, even a bookstore. At a flower stand, Agi's eyes go wide at the way bright red ocotillos and waxy yellow cactus flowers have been pulled together into a bouquet with stringy soaptree yucca leaves filling in the green. They keep walking. At a farmer's stand, they pay a small coin to refill their water jugs, and Jael restocks her pack with dried meat and bread.

In the dust of the street corner, a middle-aged woman is slapping a tight buffalo-skin drum with the palm of her hands. She's covered head to toe in more freckles than Agi has ever seen before in her life. The woman's eyes are closed, and she is caught up completely in the music flowing from her hands. She hums her shaky notes and beats her leathery fingers, and Agi sits down in front of her, legs crossed. Listening in silence, she closes her eyes to the rest of the world, and the music fills her. She doesn't notice when Jael walks away.

At the end of a song, the woman stops with her hand flat against the drum like she's searching for a pulse. The breeze lifts her hair off her face, and Agi can see her eyes are clouded over and gray. Scars crisscross over her eyelids and forehead.

"That was lovely," Agi says.

The woman snaps her head toward the sound. After a moment, she holds out the drum. "Do you want to try?"

Agi jiggles her stump, even though the woman can't see it. "I can't. I don't think there are too many one-armed drummers."

The woman reaches out for Agi's hand and pulls it to the drum. She moves their hands together, and they beat the drum. The halting rhythm smoothes as the song seeps into Agi, and eventually the old woman draws her hand away. Agi keeps drumming.

After a long while, Agi stops. The woman smiles, and Agi smiles, too.

"My name's Agi, what's yours?"

"I'm Sage," she says. The woman inclines her head toward Agi formally. "You're very good. I felt that one in my bones."

Agi laughs and pushes the drum back over to her. "Nah, I only played half the beats—the others were just bumping around in my head, wishing they had a way to get out of me."

"Well that's alright to keep a few notes inside you for a rainy day. You'll need them one day."

Agi brushes off her pants as she stands up. "Yeah, I guess so." She looks around. Jael is nowhere to be seen. "Figures," she says.

"Hmm?" Sage asks.

Agi keeps searching. "The lady I'm traveling with. She's gone. Figures. She just does things like that. She just wanders off and leaves me all the time."

"I'm sure she'll be back," Sage says.

"Maybe."

Sage's fingers tap-tap-tap the drum lightly, and Agi's eyes follow them.

"You can wait here for her if you like."

"No." Agi backs away from the woman and her drum, catching herself before she backs into a man passing hurriedly by. The man glares at her. "No, I should go look for her. It was nice to meet you, Sage."

The woman's head nods low, and the palms of her hands find the drum again with a slap-slap.

Agi takes off down the street, walking as fast as she can without running. She walks close against the sides of the buildings, as far as she can get from the crowd. The walls, mostly adobe and some old brick, feel hot on her fingertips as she drags her hand along them. The tone of Jael's voice is what Agi can't get out of her head. I said we're not talking about this. Agi scans the faces in the street, searching for tan skin, black hair.

Even when she was asking it, she knew she shouldn't. She knew she was pushing Jael away with each question she asked, but she couldn't help it. They just kept bubbling out of her.

Agi's footsteps quicken. She's jogging now. The farther she gets from the center of the city, the fewer people she sees. She practically pounces on a woman coming out of a building with long dark hair, but before she even spins around, Agi can tell it's not her.

Across the street, a man glances at Agi. He's wearing the light gray clothes of a Guard. His eyes are on her for just a moment longer than normal, and Agi turns around and walks slowly in the opposite direction. She glances over her shoulder. He's still watching. He hasn't moved, but his eyes follow her, and she breaks into a run.

23

The chain is wrapped tight around Jael's fingers, the pendant clutched in her palm. She walks through the streets, away from the girl with her too-wide eyes and the woman with the freckles and her too-loud hands.

How much does the girl know? How much has she pieced together from all the nights spent out in the desert? Jael thought—stupidly, she realizes now—that she kept the necklace out of sight at all times. She didn't think anyone else knew about it.

Her eyes scan the shops. The sooner she can get rid of it, the better.

24

Agi runs around a corner and darts into the first shop she sees. The door jingles as it slams shut behind her. It's a clothing shop. She quickly ducks behind a rack of clothes and peers to the window beyond.

"Be out in a minute!" a voice calls from somewhere in the back. Agi can't tell if it's male or female.

A sheer purple curtain covers the window, but Agi can still see the Guard when he walks quickly past. Agi smiles.

Then, she catches sight of long black hair whipping through the door to the shop across the street.

Agi picks up the corner of the purple curtain to get a better view. There's a man with a wide-brimmed hat sitting behind the counter. Jael holds her fist out to him.

It's an odd gesture. He doesn't look scared of her, so she's not starting a fight, which was Agi's first guess, knowing Jael. If anything, he looks excited. He puts his hand out under Jael's. Something glitters through her fingers when she opens them.

Agi presses her nose to the window.

The man tries to act like he doesn't really care about it, but, even from across the street, Agi can see how his fingers cling to the gold chain for dear life. The man hands over something. Jael shakes her head, and the man waves the necklace at her as he talks. Jael shakes her head again.

Finally, the man hands over more paper bills, and Jael walks out of the shop. She looks up and down the street before disappearing from Agi's view.

Agi finally turns from the window and is struck by what she sees. The clothing shop is full to the brim with fabric in every shade and texture imaginable. The type of rich, luxurious fabrics that Agi has only seen on the very, very wealthy. Colorful silk ribbons wrapped around spools line the wall to her left, and there are swatches of lace that look so delicate Agi doesn't know how they even hold themselves together. She reaches out a hand and touches a swath of bright blue fabric draped over a mannequin nearby. It's the strangest feeling—like touching running water. The label attached tells her it's something called silk.

Agi jumps when she hears feet shuffling. A large woman in a ruffley white dress is walking toward her.

"So, what can I help you with?" she asks. Her face falls when she sees Agi.

Unable to take her eyes off the woman's bright pink high heels, Agi slides toward the door. "Oh," she says, "nothing. I don't need anything. I was just looking."

The fat woman puts her hands on her hips. "Well, looking doesn't do me a lick of good. Are you going to buy something or aren't you?"

Agi's hand finds the doorknob behind her back and twists it open. A bell above her head jingles. "I'm sorry," she says. "I'll leave now."

The woman's hands fly up in the air, and she shuffles back the way she came, disappearing behind the racks of fabric.

Agi looks down the street and catches sight of Jael just as she turns a corner. She looks at the shop across the way. The sign above it reads, "Nettletown Pawn: You're selling? We're buying!"

She takes one more look in the direction Jael went and then darts across the street to the pawnshop. It is nothing like the fat lady's store. The pawnshop is full of dusty cases and ancient objects. Everywhere she looks, things gleam at her.

The man in the hat glares from behind the counter. She ducks her head and wanders to the back of the shop, pretending to be interested in a case of tall glasses and bright, clear bottles. When she glances back to the front of the shop, the man is still glaring. Agi wonders if his eyes are always so beady or if it's just when he is particularly angry. She turns back to the glasses.

She finds the cheapest one and picks it up. It slides from her fingers and falls to the floor with a tinkling crash. It's quieter than she was expecting, but still the man is beside her before she can take a breath.

"What did you do?" He's shouting.

"It just fell!" Agi backs away from the glass, bits of it crunching under her shoes.

"You stupid girl! You dropped it, didn't you?" The man is still yelling, but he walks back to the counter, grabs a hand broom, and is back beside her in a few short strides.

Agi backs up again. It crosses her mind that she's getting pretty good at walking backwards today. Then the man is shouting again, and the thought leaves her.

"Now I'm going to have to clean this up. And I'll be finding glass everywhere for weeks. And who's going to pay for it? Not you, I'm sure." The broom is old and not very effective at grabbing the tiny bits of glittering glass on the ground.

Agi sneaks to the front counter on her quietest tiptoes and grabs the diamond necklace. She slips it into her pocket, and by the time she tip-toes to the front door, the man is saying, "You're going to stay here the rest of the day and work to pay this off. Dusting and cleaning. The whole day."

Agi slowly creaks open the door. When he doesn't look up from his broom, she turns around and runs.

25

Jael is almost to the edge of the town when the girl runs up beside her. Agi watches her feet while she walks, and Jael stares straight ahead. They walk in silence toward the wavy outline of Esper in the near distance. She has no clue how the girl found her so quickly, but it doesn't matter really. The cities are just a handful of miles apart. They'll be there by nightfall.

Jael feels like she has been walking for months, but when she stops to think about it, she realizes it can't have been much more than a week. One week.

Time makes no sense anymore, Jael decides. The past few years with him felt like nothing. Not like time was flying past, but like it was simply not passing. She can remember his cough that was full of razors, but she can't remember how his hand used to feel running along the side of her chin. Right now, walking through the empty desert, she can't remember what his voice sounded like—his real voice, before he got sick. But every time she sees him, his voice is crystal clear. The house, the Bower place… It was only the drive to get rid of the necklace that kept him away in Nettletown, but still she knows somewhere in that town there is an antique shop, and he would have been waiting for her there.

He said he went there when he was a kid and it was the strangest place he'd ever seen. He said it was full of old cans made from aluminum and black boxes with colorful wires and strange plastic dolls—a huge collection of things from another world. His eyes were bright when he talked about it, and every time the story ended with Jael, I just have to take you there someday.

And just like that, the buildings of Esper start to take shape against the twilight sky. A town with no past. No memories and no future. No Cole.

Jael can almost taste it.

* * *

It's a dull, ashy sunset.

"It's going to rain," Jael says.

Agi's head jerks up. "I don't see any clouds."

"Do you see stars?"

Agi spins around, head up, almost tripping on her own feet. "No," she says.

"There you go. Clouds."

Agi squints at the town. Night has almost hidden the buildings, but they can just barely be made out.

"It's not going to rain before we get there, is it?" Agi asks.

Jael shrugs. "Probably."

"But we're so close! What are we going to do if it starts raining on us?"

Jael looks over. "We'll get wet, Agi. It won't be the end of the world."

"But where are we going to sleep?"

"In town. You'll be in a nice warm bed at your aunt's."

Agi bites her lip. "Umm." She cuts her eyes over to Jael. "Umm, we have to talk about something." She stops walking, looks up at the gray sky.

Jael stops too and turns to face her. Her pulse quickens. The girl knows something. About the fires, about Cole, about her. The Bower farm was her mistake. The Guards will be after her now. Jael's hands clench into fists.

For a minute, Agi doesn't say anything. The moment stretches, and a coyote howls. Agi glances nervously over her shoulder, and when she turns around again, her eyes don't quite meet Jael's.

"What?" Jael says finally.

Agi's eyes jump to Jael and then back down to her feet. "Umm," she starts, "I might not have told you everything about my aunt."

Relief floods over Jael. She doesn't know. Then suspicion creeps back in. "What didn't you tell me?"

The sky is getting darker by the minute, and Jael can barely make out Agi's outline. Her hand fiddles with the tattered hem of her shirt. "I don't know exactly where she lives."

Jael furrows her brow. "So you'll go into town and ask around for her. I'm sure you'll find her."

Agi nods slowly. "Yeah," she says in a small voice.

A big fat raindrop lands on Jael's shoulder. It's cool and deliciously wet, but Jael keeps her eyes on Agi. There's something more. "What?" she asks.

Agi jerks her head up and holds her palm out. "It's raining," she says.

Jael wipes water from her forehead before it drips down into her eyes. "What else, Agi?"

Agi pulls her bag onto the top of her head and balances it with her arm. She looks like a turtle with wild strawberry hair. "We're going to get soaked."

The rain is falling faster now, the drops thick and heavy.

"Agi," Jael says shortly.

Agi bites her lip once more. And then it all spills out. "I don't know where she lives at all. I mean, I think I have an aunt, somewhere, but I don't know what town she lives in."

Jael blinks and water falls into her eyes. She rubs it away. Her hair weighs heavily against her neck, drenched. "So you were lying," she says. "When you said you were going to Esper. That was a lie."

Agi shakes her head, and her bag falls down onto her shoulders again. "No—I mean yes—I mean, I knew I was going somewhere, I just didn't know where. I just named the first town that popped into my head and got lucky, I guess, that you were going there too."

Agi realizes she's rambling and stops. She watches Jael. Jael tries to piece together her thoughts. Her stomach twists. She's so close—a step away from finally being free. Does it really have to change anything? She was going to leave the girl in town anyway. That was the plan all along.

In the now pitch-black sky, thunder crashes.

"I'm not seeing the problem," Jael says finally.

Agi tilts her head. "I don't have anywhere to go."

"I don't see the problem for me," Jael clarifies. Her face is calm, but inside everything is screaming. She's so close. The girl doesn't know anything about her, not really. Not about the fires. She just needs to get away. Just cut the cord. The girl can find her own way from here.

Agi's mouth hangs open. Thunder rolls again. "You can't just leave me."

A headache builds at the base of Jael's skull, on top of everything else. She doesn't say anything, just stares at the girl.

"You can't," Agi says. Then screaming, "You can't!" Her voice is high-pitched and unnatural.

All Jael can think about is how to get away. If she just starts running—right now—will the girl follow?

"I don't even know you," Jael says.

At first, Agi is stunned. Then her features turn angular. "Well, I know plenty about you," she spits.

Lightning shakes the sky, and water cascades down Jael's back and arms and face.

"I know enough, at least." Agi walks a step forward, fearless with anger. "I know you burned down that field. You thought I was asleep, but I wasn't, and I followed and saw. You burned it all down. And I know about Cole."

Jael notices with an odd sense of detachment that she's standing in water. Was she always standing in water?

"I know how you act like you're all sad and everything because he's dead. But I know."

Jael watches Agi's lips move, and the sound of the words comes to her a second later.

"I know you killed him. You talk in your sleep. Screaming about it every night. Screaming."

There's some sort of pressure tugging on Jael's ankles. When she looks down, she all of a sudden can't remember where she is. It looks like she's standing in the middle of a river, fast moving and dangerous. Her mind is sluggish to make sense of what she's seeing, but eventually the words bubble to the surface. Flash flood.

The rain is coming down in sheets, but the desert is not made to hold so much water. It's up above her ankles.

"We've got to get out of here." Jael spins around, trying to see through the dark, trying to find some sort of high ground.

Agi doesn't move. "Did you hear what I said?"

Jael holds her hands above her eyes to block the rain, and—the lightning strikes—she sees it. Off to her left, the land slopes up into a small hill. If the water keeps rising, it won't be enough, but it's all they have.

"This way," she says to the girl. She's surprised by how calm her voice is.

Agi still doesn't move. "No," she says. "I'm not going with you anymore. You killed him, didn't you?"

The scent in the air has shifted. The smell of wet dust and mud and, very faintly, Juniper.

"Aren't you going to say anything?"

Jael doesn't turn around. The girl knows. It's over. His voice, even now, whispers in her ear. She can't make out the words, or maybe it's just the wind, but either way.

"What do you want me to say?"

The swift water forces Agi sideways a few steps. It's up to her knees.

Jael expects the girl to yell, but her voice is small, barely audible over the rain. "Tell me you were just dreaming. Tell me it was just a nightmare. Tell me it wasn't you that burned down that house I was living in."

"I didn't have a choice," Jael says.

Agi looks at her. She tilts her head, trying to process Jael's words. Lightning dashes the sky with electric green sparks, and the girl jumps. Her feet lose their grip on the slippery ground, and she lands on her back, the water almost overtaking her.

Jael just watches as she pushes herself to her feet. Agi leans to the right to counter the flow of water and watches Jael. In the darkness, Jael can see nothing of her expression.

Lightning strikes again, this time illuminating the hill. Jael walks toward it.

And Agi follows.

* * *

The walking is hard, and halfway there Agi's feet are swept from beneath her again. When she stands up, water pours from the bottom of her bag like a waterfall. By the time they make it to the base of the hill, the water is up to Agi's waist and shows no sign of slowing.

At the top of the hill, Agi plops down immediately. Anger and fear and pain course through her veins until her system is overloaded. Jael can hear sniffling for hours as the rain pours on, but finally it sounds as though the girl has fallen asleep.

At another bolt of lightning, Jael spots the town, closer than she thought. Probably less than an hour's walk away, if there weren't so much water.

The sky lights up again, and he's there—beside her—watching.

She closes her eyes.

* * *

When she opens her eyes again, the rain has stopped. The moon has finally risen, and everything is gray.

Jael digs through her bag. Everything is soaked.

Her hands shake as she pulls out her matchbook. Each slender piece of wood, so delicate and so dangerous, is drenched. She curses under her breath.

Then she sees it. In the middle of all the others, one small match sits unbroken, its sulfur tip inexplicably dry. Jael takes this as a good sign.

The blue is what always surprises her the most. She expects the crackling red and screaming orange as the fire catches. The brightness of it burns her eyes, but it too is no surprise.

What she always forgets about is the way the match strikes blue like sea foam and sky. It is in those few milliseconds that time freezes. That she stops to question.

She looks down. Agi's body is tightly curled and smaller in sleep.

Cole's voice in her ear. "*I always said you would make a good mom.*"

She can't see him, but she can hear him, can hear the smile on his lips.

"*You never believed me.*"

Jael stares at the little speck of fire under her control. Now the little girl's sleeping body shivers in the cold night air, just like his body shivered in pain so many nights. And now, in the violent shadows cast by the flickering match, her hair looks dark like his.

The girl knows everything. As soon as they reach town, the girl will turn her in and the Guards will be after her, and she'll be hunted wherever she goes, and, worse than all that, when she looks down at the sleeping girl now, all she can see is him. She can't get away.

Jael wonders if the blanket is too wet to catch.

She feels his breath on the back of her neck.

"*Shhh,*" *he says.*

The match's heat trickles closer to her fingertips. Somewhere in the distance she hears a rushing. She looks up. The sound is getting closer, louder. Someone is coming.

No. It's the wind. She tries to see it, to see anything at all, but she cannot. She pictures it instead: the wind rustling through the desert, its fingers running roughly over everything, hoarding textures like a cactus hoards water. Where she stands, the air is still. But it's coming closer.

Jael with the match, Agi curled tightly into herself. Together and separate, they await.

The wind arrives. A sudden gust grabs the match, and the flame puffs out. A thin whisper of gray-blue smoke curls up to the moon.

His voice again, "*Shh.*" *Softly,* "*Shh.*"

Agi turns over in her sleep and tugs the blanket higher on her shoulders. She snuggles her hand under her chin.

Jael runs.

26

Jael runs blindly, water sloshing, each step a struggle to stay upright. When she gets to Esper, she doesn't stop. The city is even bigger than Nettletown, and it doesn't take long before she's completely lost in the maze of streets. Still she runs, whipping around corners, turning at random, sometimes retracing her own steps. She runs with fire on her heels. She runs until the sky turns gray with approaching dawn, and then she runs until the sun blazes above the desert skyline. She runs until the broken glass windows in the buildings catch fire from the sun and turn orange with reflected light.

She runs until she falls.

* * *

Midmorning, Jael wakes with her back stiff and aching. Her head throbs. She looks around and spots a dark patch where blood has dried on a rock beside her. She must have hit her head when she tripped.

The memory of last night comes back to her all in a rush. The flood, the fight. Agi.

She pushes it away. There's nothing more to be done. She had to be rid of the girl one way or another. That's what all this has been about, right? She's finally here. Esper. The city with absolutely nothing to remind her of him. A fresh start.

She gets up slowly, fighting to keep her vision in focus, and looks around. The city is not what she was expecting. Remnants of the old world peek out in unexpected places. Pre-fallout buildings are mostly still standing, but people have begun building up. On top of the old frames, second, third, and even fourth floors have been added. It makes Jael dizzy to look up at them.

She looks down instead. Beside her is a perfect circle in the ground. She peers inside and sees the sewer beneath. She wonders why someone hasn't covered it up. It would be easy to fall in. People walk by one after the other, none so much as glancing her way. They must have been stepping over her for hours. She could have died right there, her body slowly eaten by ravens and dust beetles, and these people would have kept stepping over her, too busy to stop and push her into an alley to decompose in peace. Fine, she thinks. They don't need her, and she certainly doesn't need them. She stands stiffly, watching the people flow by.

Then someone in the crowd stops abruptly. People hurry around him, water curving seamlessly around a rock.

Even from this distance, it's his eyes that catch her off guard.

Haskell's hands are clenched into fists, his shoulders up by his ears. The right side of his head is scored like a loaf of bread. Jael takes a step back reflexively. Her back presses into brick. With the sun still on the other side of the building, the bricks are surprisingly cool.

Before she can form a plan, he has crossed the street and stands right in front of her.

She puts her hands up to keep him at bay, and his right hand locks tightly around her wrist. His left arm hangs loosely at his side, the skin pink and brown and open around the elbow.

"You," he rasps, "Are not an easy person to keep up with."

Dark circles shadow his eyes, and his chin is covered in scruff.

Jael twists her hand free from his grip, but he grabs her other arm just as she starts to run away.

Jael feels something cold against her stomach. She looks down to see Haskell's oddly bent left arm holding a knife against her. She can feel the coolness of the metal through her shirt.

She freezes. At a slightly different angle, the knife would be in her stomach instead of against it. She feels her own knife along the inside edge of her boot, but bending to get it would shift that angle distinctly not in her favor.

"How did you find me?" she asks, hoping to buy some time.

He switches the knife to his good hand, letting go of his grip on her arm. "Don't you remember? You told me right where to find you."

He keeps the knife low with his broad back blocking it from view. Jael wonders what would happen if she just cried out. No one makes eye contact with her as they pass by.

"All I had to do was wait," he continues.

The pressure on her stomach strengthens. His eyes are hungry as he says, "Now give me the necklace."

She knows before she says it that he won't believe her. Still, she says, "I don't have it."

He pushes the knife, and she gasps. She looks down, and the blood is bright red on her shirt in a perfect circle, spreading slowly out.

"Don't lie. I know you have it. You would still be there digging through the dirt if you hadn't found it."

She puts her hands against his shoulders, trying to push him away, but he's too strong and he won't budge. "I don't have it!"

He jerks the neck of her shirt to the side, looking for the bright gold chain. She stretches her hand desperately toward her boot, but it's too far. She can't reach.

"The girl has it, doesn't she? Where is she?" He keeps his knife pressed against her while he scans the street over his shoulders. The blade stings her skin. His eyes are so wild. Jael wonders how she ever could have thought they looked like Cole's.

While his head is turned, Jael strikes.

Her fist lands in the soft flesh of his neck, and he drops the knife to the ground, clutching his throat and gasping for air.

She doesn't wait to see what he does next. Jael runs faster than she has ever run before, away from his coughing and rasping and choking sounds. She turns corners blindly, frantically trying to put as much distance and as many buildings between them as she can. She hears footsteps behind her. At each turn, she looks over her shoulder.

Finally, she sees him.

She whips her head forward to look at the street she's just turned onto.

It's a dead end. A tall wooden building blocks her path at the end of the street. She runs until she reaches it, feeling the wood wall, trying to convince herself it's not real, it's not real, she can keep running. But she can't.

There's nowhere left to go.

She hears his steps down the alley. He's no longer running.

Still looking at the wall, she reaches down and tugs her knife from where she has it strapped in the lining of her boot.

She grips it tightly and then, heart hammering, turns to face him.

"Where is the girl?" he asks. He keeps walking toward her.

"I don't know." Jael says. "I left her last night after—It doesn't matter. She doesn't have it."

Haskell stops walking a few yards away from her.

"I sold it," she says.

His eyebrows turn up at the edges. "Then you must have a whole lot of money in that bag."

She clutches the strap of her backpack. It's her chance to start over. To find someplace new. Someplace quiet. To forget. It's her only chance.

Haskell points his knife at her. "Hand it over."

She slowly lifts her hand and points her knife at him.

His eyes flick to it, and his eyebrows shoot up. For just one moment, she thinks it's an expression of fear. But then he laughs.

One short, loud bark from his chest. "Hah! You came prepared this time, didn't you?" He smiles. "But let me ask you something."

It's a wicked smile, and it sends a shiver down Jael's arms.

"All this running. Do you actually think you can escape what you're running from?"

Her cheeks flush red from the sudden wave of anger. Hatred. Revulsion. She's not sure all of it is for him. He chuckles under his breath.

Then he rushes toward her; she rears back and hurls her knife, the blade flipping over and over and over until it stops with a thud. His knife falls from his hands, clattering on the ground.

Blood rushes from his chest, and he stumbles forward, catching himself on her shoulders.

She hears the blood hit the ground.

Sees his eyes widen in shock.

His hands grip her for a moment before he falls to his knees, then his side, then his back. The brown handle—now red—sticks out from his chest, just below his rib cage.

Jael's vision is turning black, and she leans heavily against the building behind her, desperately trying to pull air into her flattened lungs. She looks at him again. His eyes are wide open and blank, staring emptily up at the sky.

She doubles over and vomits.

Then, for the last time, Jael runs.

27

Cole runs beside her, his footsteps falling exactly in time with her own. She pushes herself faster, faster, faster, but she can't outrun him. She doesn't need to look to know that he is there. She can picture the way his sweat collects on his brow and on the tops of his shoulders and the way his fists are tight, elbows in by his sides as he runs.

A few people actually turn to look at her as she runs, their expressions curious. It's not until she reaches another dead end that she realizes why. She reaches out to lean heavily on a metal fence at the end of an alley, and her hands are dark red and crusted with blood. It's on her stomach, too. She lifts up her shirt, and the small red line grins at her.

She can feel Cole standing behind her.

"Why won't you leave me alone?" she whispers to the fence. He doesn't answer.

She has to get away. He's too close, and he's not there at all. Just like at the end. She clutches her hands to her temples.

To her left, there is a door.

The padlock is rusty orange, and the wood is almost rotten through. Still, she is surprised by the amount of effort it takes to kick in.

She's standing in an abandoned warehouse. It looks like it used to be some sort of factory with giant wooden beams spread throughout the room, supporting the ceiling. A dozen giant machines with their wheels and levers and belts picked bare fill the space. Tall, empty shelves lean against the walls.

She slams the door back in its frame, but when she spins around he is still there, standing in front of her, watching.

She can't get away.

His hair looks so soft, and all she wants to do is run her hands through it and press her face into his neck. What does he smell like? She can't remember.

She takes a step forward.

Another.

Then she blinks, and he's standing right in front of her. She inhales. She smells nothing. Her hand stretches toward his deep black hair, but then she blinks again, and he is halfway across the room.

She takes a deep breath and walks to him again, reaching for the matchbook in her back pocket at the same time.

As she gets closer, he vanishes. She whips around, and he is right behind her. Then beside her. Now across the room. Now in front of her, close enough to kiss. She leans forward, and he's gone again.

She's crying now. He's always there and never there, and she can't get away. Her fingers fumble for a match, but, when she strikes the sulfur tip, nothing happens.

Her heart skips a beat.

She strikes another, then another. Nothing. Then she remembers—the rainstorm—the flood—the last match—Agi. Everything ruined.

Agi.

Suddenly she can see Agi too, standing by Cole, smiling at her.

Jael squeezes her eyes shut. She strikes each match, hoping against hope that one of them will catch. Her skin itches with the need to find one that will light, anything to push away the shadows.

Down to the last match. Strike. Nothing.

She opens her eyes. They're looking at her.

She scans the room wildly for something that she can use, but everything blurs and spins around her. One moment she sees the room in front of her, and the next she's looking down at Haskell's empty eyes and all that red. Then Agi is beside her, twirling in a circle with her arm outstretched. If only she still had her knife. Or just one good match. She'd only need one.

At some point Jael's hair fell out of its knot, and it hangs now in front of her face. Through the thick black strands, a gleam of light catches her eye. A clear broken bottle leans in a corner. The jagged glass edges peek out from the shadows.

She does not remember standing up, walking across the room, or bending down to pick it up, but she must have done all these things because the bottle now sits in her dark red hands.

She expected to feel hopeful. She felt a desperate hope when she held the matches moments ago, but now she feels nothing. Cole sits with his head leaning against the wall as he watches her. Agi has disappeared.

The sunlight falls through the windows in bright, hot squares. Jael drags some dry wood from a corner and sits down in a patch of sun. She gathers a few scraps of paper, tearing them into tiny strips. She wipes the dust from the bottle and twists the curved edge this way and that. The sun plays on the glass until she finds the best angle.

It takes a few minutes, but finally smoke curls up from the paper in thin tendrils. She holds her hand steady, and soon a flame bursts out of the smoke. It is bright and strong. She quickly leans two pieces of wood over the flame and they catch.

Even though there is no wind, Jael cups her hand around the flame tenderly as she carries the wood over to one of the tall shelves against the wall. She watches until the flames jump up from the wood onto the lowest shelf. Then she walks over to Cole and sits next to him. When she looks, her arm is touching his.

She wishes she could feel it. She wishes she could lean her head on his shoulder.

It's not perfect, but it's done.

28

Agi smells it before she sees it. Smoke.

That's when she notices she's swimming upstream. Everyone is hurrying in the other direction. Some are running. Her stomach jumps into her throat as she turns around and walks, then runs, toward the column of smoke a few streets over. When she rounds the corner, the flames are bright orange and shooting out of the roof, and she knows.

A crowd of people stands on the far side of the street, and a smaller group forms a bucket line pouring water bit by bit onto the burning building.

"That's never going to work." Agi says it to herself, but a lady standing beside her in a flowered dress and matching hat answers.

"It'll work," she says. "I've seem 'em do it before. That one there is my Elex." She points. "He knows what he's doing. It might take 'em awhile, but they'll get it done." The lady sounds weirdly proud, like this fire is a competition and her son is going to win first prize.

Agi watches the last man in the line. Each bucket hisses on the flames. It's like trying to kill an elephant with a toothpick.

"How are they going to get the people out?"

This time the flowered lady doesn't hear. She is facing a younger woman on her other side, talking excitedly with her hands. Agi pulls on her arm.

"The people inside?" she asks again.

The woman waves a dismissive hand at Agi. "That building's been empty forty years. No one in there but the rats, and Lord knows we could stand to lose a few of them."

Agi's stomach flips.

The front door is blocked by the annoyingly small bucket line, but on the other side of the building the street cuts away into an alley.

Agi looks at the faces around her. Each one is turned to watch the slow firefighting. When she's sure no one is looking, she darts across the side street and into the alley.

The heat is strong so close to the building. There's an open hole in the side where it looks like a door, and maybe part of the wall, has fallen in. Thick black smoke pours from the opening, but Agi can't see any flames. She takes a deep breath and runs inside.

The deep breath was a bad idea. The air outside was already full of smoke, and Agi immediately starts coughing and can't stop. Between the smoke stinging her eyes and her violent coughing, she can't see anything but smoke and, deeper in the room, fire.

"Jael?" she yells between bouts of coughing.

No answer.

Something crashes on her left, and she jumps as a huge wooden beam falls from the ceiling. It's bright with flames, and she can feel the scorching heat on her skin. She stumbles back from it. Then another beam crashes behind her, blocking the door.

"Jael!" she yells again.

She's starting to feel light-headed. The room is getting darker, even as more fire falls down from the ceiling in sparkling chunks.

She realizes she's standing next to a tall shelf that's not yet on fire, and she squeezes between it and the wall, trying to take cover from the raining flames.

She calls out again, as loud as she can, "Jael!" It uses every ounce of oxygen left in her lungs.

29

Someone is calling her name. She's sure of it. It is a voice she used to know, or at least she feels like she has heard it before.

She opens her eyes and looks beside her. There's no one there. Was someone supposed to be there? Her head throbs.

A small voice from far away. "Jael!"

It's that voice again, calling her name. A crash. She waits to see if she'll hear it again, but it doesn't come. The room spins around her. It's too bright. Why is it so bright and so dark at the same time?

The pieces fall into place, one at a time. Fire. Smoke. The glass bottle, and Cole, and Haskell, and the girl—

Her muscles are leaden. She was so close to being asleep. She shuts her eyes again, but the voice is still there. Fainter, now.

"Jael!"

The little girl with one arm. Agi.

What is she doing here? After everything that's happened, the girl is here. Again. Why is Agi putting up with all of this? Why is she chasing after what is so clearly a hopeless case? She knows about Cole and the fires and everything, and yet she's here.

No matter what, she just keeps following.

Something crashes. Agi's voice breaks off mid-cry.

"Agi!" Jael's voice comes out as a whisper. Her throat feels like it's been screaming for days. She tries again. "Agi!" This time it's a little louder.

But there's no answer.

Jael pushes herself to her feet and hobbles toward the crash she heard earlier. The room spins. Her skin is oddly dry, without a drop of sweat, and it crosses her mind that this is a very bad sign.

A wooden ceiling beam has fallen onto a shelf tilted against the wall, and the whole thing is extraordinarily on fire. Agi's legs peek out from behind it all, inches from the flames.

The room spins more violently around Jael.

She grabs Agi's feet and tugs hard, sliding her from behind the shelf. Just as Jael is about to faint from relief that she is not burned, a flame catches on her wild strawberry hair.

Jael pulls her farther away and stamps on her hair, pounding the flame into the ground before it can climb to her scalp. The acrid scent of burnt hair mixes in with the smoke. Behind them, another piece of roof crashes to the ground. The room is too bright with all the fire.

Jael scoops Agi up and throws her over her shoulder. She looks for the door to the alley, but it's blocked by a wall of flame. It crosses her mind, at that moment, that she didn't stop to see if Agi was breathing.

She searches frantically for another way out. Everywhere she looks: fire, smoke, wall. Then she notices the smoke flowing in a trail away from her, toward the other side of the building.

A door.

Jael swings Agi into her arms, holding her as close to her chest as possible. She veers around the burning pieces of roof, winding a way across the impossibly long room.

The door is open—she can see distant, hazy, smoke-filled sky beyond it. They're so close.

A flaming shingle drops from the ceiling and lands on her shoulder. She screams as it sears through her shirt and into her flesh. She drops Agi on the ground as she falls.

Jael swats the fire until her shoulder is no longer burning, though her skin is bright pink and black.

She can't lift her right arm; the burned shoulder refuses to move, so she awkwardly hoists Agi up with one arm and carries her against her side.

Seven slow steps and then—they're out. The smoke is thick, and the heat is everywhere, rolling through the air in waves. But they're out.

Jael sees a handful of men running toward them.

Then her arms feel oddly light, pavement fills her vision, an explosion of fireworks, and she's gone.

30

Jael is at the bottom of the ocean. Lights and warbly sounds drift down to her slowly. The water pushes on her head until the pressure makes it feel disconnected from her body. Almost. The pain in her shoulder stands as a stark contrast to the numbness of the rest of her body. A million tiny knives stabbing.

Then she can no longer breathe. She's at the bottom of the ocean, and she's out of oxygen. Her heart races as she swims to the top.

Jael wakes with the sun in her face. She gulps down huge mouthfuls of air. For a long moment, she thinks she is outside, but her eyes slowly focus on the window in front of her. It's open wide and a breeze drifts over to her. She's lying on a thin mattress.

She's in a room that is noisy and unfamiliar and also very big. A Relief Center, she realizes. There are a dozen or so small metal beds, about half of which are occupied. Relief workers are scattered about the room, reading charts and fiddling about in cabinets. Jael turns her head to the side to try and see the end of the room, but the movement causes the room to spin, so she shuts her eyes and tries to lie very still. The air smells strongly of peppermint.

"Look who's awake."

Someone touches Jael's wrist, causing her to jump. She takes deep breaths to swallow down the nausea before opening her eyes.

A young woman looks down at her. She has round silver glasses perched on the tip of her nose and a band with a red cross on her arm.

"Didn't mean to startle you," the relief worker says.

Jael starts to say something, but her tongue feels cottony and too big for her mouth. She can't make it move in the right patterns for speech.

"Don't try to talk," the woman says. "You got a bad concussion when you fell."

Jael tries to remember a fall. Her head is still floating directionless in the current. It's hard to steer.

"Do you remember what happened?"

Jael shakes her head, very minutely. She feels she's been sleeping for a long time, but she also has a feeling that she's very glad she woke up.

"That's okay. It will come back to you. The Healer says there shouldn't be any permanent damage." She puts her hand back on Jael's wrist, lightly. "You were in a fire. All anybody saw was the flames going up and then you running out with that girl in your arms—"

"Agi." Jael sits up, and the room flips upside down. She collapses back down. The woman puts a hand on her shoulder to keep her there.

"The girl is fine," she says. "Left here a few days ago, actually, in quite a hurry. Said she had an aunt or something to get to." The woman tsks.

Jael's thoughts are moving faster now. A few days. She could be anywhere. She forces her mouth to speak through the cotton. "I've got to find her."

The woman shrugs. "I asked her if she wanted to wait around for you, but she said she'd better get going. She said to tell you thanks though, as if that means much. She told us what happened. It was real brave of you to go in that building to save her. I still don't know what she was doing in there in the first place. She said she was exploring—who knows why—and the fire started out of nowhere." She wags a finger at Jael. "Something suspicious with that one, if you ask me. Anyways, she didn't even stick around to make sure you were alright." The woman shakes her head and pushes her glasses up on her nose. "Kids."

When Jael doesn't say anything, the woman takes this as a sign of disappointment. "It's okay." She pats Jael's arm. "Everyone knows you're the hero." She walks to the other side of the bed and bends over Jael's other arm. "How's the shoulder feel?"

Jael just shakes her head.

"I'll put some more cream on it."

The knives stab deeper as the nurse pulls back the bandage covering her shoulder. Jael grits her teeth. The peppermint smell grows stronger. It's coming from a jar of thick white cream in the woman's hands, which she spreads gingerly over Jael's raw skin. Surprisingly, her touch doesn't hurt. The cream smoothes out the edges of the pain, leaving behind a steady ache that Jael can deal with. She exhales deeply.

The woman smiles and twists the lid back on the jar. "Good stuff, isn't it? You're lucky. We've got the best Healer in town."

Jael closes her eyes, and her breathing evens out. One final pat on her arm and then footsteps as the nurse click-clacks away.

31

When Jael opens her eyes again, it is night. Everything is quiet. Her head is significantly clearer, but the pain from her shoulder is what woke her. The peppermint jar sits on a small table beside her bed, so she peels back the bandage and smoothes some more cream over the wound. She looks at the jar. It is a large container, and it's still almost full. Enough for weeks.

When she stands, her muscles react slowly, but at least the room doesn't spin so much.

She looks a moment for her bag, but then it hits her. All that money burned to nothing. Somehow, that seems fitting.

She grabs the jar and peers into the dim moonlit room, but there's only one relief worker, and he is fast asleep in a chair by the door. He doesn't stir as she slips past him into the cool desert air.

The buildings in this part of town have all been torn down and rebuilt from hodge-podged bits of wood and metal. Some of them lean a little, but they're still standing.

Almost immediately someone runs toward her. Before Jael's sluggish mind can process the danger, she sees that the person is small with a wild mane of curly hair flying behind her.

Agi runs like she's going to hurdle straight into Jael, but she pulls up short a few yards away.

"Are you okay?"

"They said you left," Jael says.

Agi shrugs. "Are you okay?"

Jael nods.

For a long moment Agi says nothing. Then in a small voice, "Really?" There's a dark bruise on her arm, and her hair is singed and uneven.

A hundred images flash through Jael's brain, but her mind finally settles on one: Agi, eyes bright, ear bent close to the sagebrush, listening to the wind blow through the paper leaves.

"Yeah," Jael says. "Let's go."

Agi doesn't ask where, and Jael is glad because she doesn't know. Jael starts walking, and Agi follows.

* * *

Before they can make it out of town, Jael's bruised body starts to slow down. Her shoulder throbs, and her head feels sluggish. They find an empty shell of a building, and in the back is a door marked "Stairs" in chipped red letters. Agi shoves the door open and leads them all the way up to the roof.

Agi walks right to the edge of the building and plops down with her feet dangling over the side. Jael sits on the flat roof a few feet back. The moon is low in the west, so it must be past midnight. The town is covered in darkness, but the noises drift up. Voices muttering, feet shuffling, something clinking. It's a big town, and people move about restlessly.

Agi pulls something from her pocket. The gold chain sparkles in the moonlight as she holds it out to Jael.

"You shouldn't have sold it." She shakes it at Jael. "It was his, wasn't it? He gave it to you?"

Jael's eyes are locked on the necklace.

Agi leans over and shakes it at Jael again. "Take it."

Jael's eyes drift from the diamond to Agi's face. Agi's eyes are wide and, in this weird light, look almost gray. "You keep it."

At first, Agi doesn't move. Then when Jael doesn't say anything else, she slowly pulls her arm in to her chest, clutching the necklace. She has to wrangle the chain over her disorderly hair, but she eventually gets it into place. It hangs down almost to her belly button.

Though her thoughts are slow, Jael starts to plan. She doesn't know where they'll go or how they'll eat or where they'll sleep tomorrow night. Past the buildings, the desert stretches in front of them, endless and washed-out in the moonlight. She needs to start somewhere, so she brushes the dirt away from a section of the roof and gestures Agi toward it. Then she brushes the dirt from another section a few feet away and lies down, curled up on her good shoulder.

Eventually, Agi lies down. Her eyes find Jael's for a moment. Then she rolls onto her back and looks up at the stars. Jael finds herself wishing she could remember the names of them so she could point them out to Agi. Cole was always trying to teach them to her, but they never sank in.

Jael looks up at the clear sky and breathes deep. Her skin feels dry and itchy. She wishes it would rain again, but she knows that only happens once in a blue moon in the desert. The wind brushes her hair from her face, and it sounds like *shhhh*.

She knows that the nightmares will come back, if not tonight then another night. The flames and the dark blood and the jagged feel of cracked lungs. But as she falls asleep, she's not thinking of any of that. As Jael drifts off, she's thinking of how his nose always crinkled when he smiled and of what he would say if he were here now. Suddenly she remembers—Gemini. The crooked line of stars above her head, shaped like two twins holding hands. Such a funny name.

She looks over to tell Agi, but she's already asleep. She'll have to tell her in the morning.

Abbey Lenzie is a writer from Huntsville, Alabama. After studying creative writing and film at Birmingham-Sourthern College, she moved to Los Angeles with her husband. Her passions include eating fried okra, crocheting blankets, and identifying plants with field guides.

The cover artwork was done by Christian Dellavedona. Christian is an italian illustrator. He lives in Milan where he works as freelancer on editorial and advertising projects for italian and foreign clients. (partial client list: The Boston Globe, Reader's Digest, Print Magazine, Wired, National Journal, Time Out, Strategy+Business, Men's Journal, Men's Health, Entrerpreneur Magazine, Canadian Business, Park Slope Reader, NY Spirit, Internazionale, Aspen Institute, Radiotimes, TBWA, Il Sole 24 Ore, Mondadori, RCS, Cairo Editore, Marsilio, Baldini Castoldi, Eni).

Eliza Vasquez is a writer and editor, holding a BA in English and a minor in Film & TV Studies from California State University, Fullerton. She was a part of this year's Plaza Literary Prize Committee, and is currently working within The Walt Disney Company. She is intending to pursue a career in the publishing industry while editing and publishing her own novel. When she isn't at Disney, you can find her volunteering for *MuggleNet.com*.

Christina Ramos is a writer and editor holding a BA in English with an emphasis in writing. She plans on earning her Master's Degree by 2020. She intends to pursue a career in editing within the book publishing industry. She is an avid reader fiction and writes it herself in her spare time. Her dream is to publish her own novel or collection of short stories. When she is not editing, reading or writing, she can be found volunteering at her local church or spending quality time with family and friends.

Special thanks to The Plaza Literary Prize 2018 Committee including: Eliza Vasquez, Christina Ramos, Marina Shugrue, Hannah Fierheller, Jordan Tharp, Joy Taylor, and Dennis Corbett.

1888 is a tax-exempt organization under section 501(c)(3) of the Internal Revenue Code. Donations are tax deductible to the extent allowed by law. Employer Identification Number (EIN): 47-4550601

Made in the USA
Columbia, SC
20 February 2019